RYAN'S HIS NAME, BUT THEY CALL HIM

THE HOOD—

A big, ugly sonofabitch with a blistering temper, a college education and a sizzling record of convictions for assault, robbery and murder. He's the kind of bad news you steer clear of— unless you're a woman. The Hood knows his way around the corruption jungle, and he's met all the animals— from two-bit killers and strung-out hookers to the biggest czars in the International Syndicate. Now he's hired out to the cops for the highest price the Department's ever paid: *carte blanche to kill.*

The Hood stalks his prey through the brutal, bloody world of big-city crime in two complete new Spillane blockbusters, ME, HOOD! and RETURN OF THE HOOD

Other SIGNET Thrillers
by Mickey Spillane

◎ ◎ ◎ ◎ ◎

ME, HOOD !

◎ ◎ ◎ ◎ ◎

By
MICKEY SPILLANE

A SIGNET BOOK

Published by
THE NEW AMERICAN LIBRARY

SIGNET TRADEMARK REG. U.S. PAT. OFF. AND FOREIGN COUNTRIES
REGISTERED TRADEMARK—MARCA REGISTRADA
HECHO EN CHICAGO, U.S.A.

SIGNET BOOKS are published by
The New American Library, Inc.,
1301 Avenue of the Americas, New York, New York 10019

FIRST PRINTING, JANUARY, 1969

PRINTED IN THE UNITED STATES OF AMERICA

CONTENTS

ME, HOOD!

THEY picked me up in a bar on Second Avenue and waited for the supper crowd to flow out before they made their tap, two tall smiling lads with late model narrow-brim Kellys that helped them blend into the background of young junior executives.

But both of them had that almost imperceptible cock to their arms that comes from wearing a gun too long on one side, and that made them something else again.

When they came in they pulled out stools on either side of me and began the routine, but I saved them all the trouble they had planned to go to. I finished my drink, pocketed my change and stood up. "We go now?"

Without changing the size of his smile the one with the pale blue eyes said, "We go now."

I grinned, nodded toward the bartender and walked to the door. On the street a gentle nudge edged me north, then another turned me at the corner to where the car was parked. One got behind the wheel and one was on my right. I didn't feel any gun rubbing against my hip where it should have, so I knew the guy on my right had it in his hand.

At the door the squat little man stood with his legs spraddled and hands in his pockets, looking at nothing, yet watching everything. The other one sat on the window ledge at my shoulder without saying anything.

Across the city the clock on the square boomed nine. Behind me the door to the inside office opened and a voice said, "Bring him in."

Smiling Boy let me go ahead of him, followed me in and closed the door.

Then, for the first time, I was wishing I hadn't played the wise guy. I felt like an idiot for being so damn dumb and while I was trying to put it together I could feel the coldness creeping over me like a winter fog. I shut my mouth and grinned so I wouldn't start sounding off and let them see the hate I wore like my own skin.

Cops. Out of uniform, but cops. Five in front, one behind me. Two more in the room outside. There was something different about the five, though. The mold was the same, but the metal seemed tempered. If there were any cutting edges they were well hidden, yet ready to expose themselves as fast as a switch blade.

Five men in various shades of single-breasted blues and greys with solemn dark ties on white that hinted at formality not found in general police work. Five pairs of expressionless, yet scrutinizing eyes that somehow seemed weathered and not too easily amused.

But the thin one at the end of the table was different, and I watched him deliberately and knew he was hating my guts just as hard as I was hating his.

From his place at the door, Smiling Boy said, "He knew us. He was waiting for us."

The thin one's voice had a flat quality to it. "You think much for . . . a punk."

"I'm not the kind of punk you're used to."

"How long have you known?"

I shrugged. "Since you started." I told him, "Two weeks."

They looked at each other, annoyed, some angry. One leaned forward on the desk, his face flushed. "How did you know?"

"I told you. I'm no ordinary punk."

". . . I asked you a question."

I looked at the guy at the table. His hands were tight and white at the knuckles, but his face had lost its flush. "I've been a while at this game myself," I said. "Every animal knows it's got a tail no matter how short it is. I knew I had mine the first day you tacked it on."

The guy looked past me to Smiling Boy. "Did you know that?"

My buddy at the door fidgeted a second, then: "No, sir."

"Was it ever suspected?"

Another hesitation. "No, sir. None of the reports from the other shifts mentioned it."

"Great," the man said, "just great." Then he looked back at me again. "You could have shaken this tail?"

"Anytime."

"I see." He paused and sucked his lip into his teeth. "But you preferred not to. Why?"

"Let's say I was curious."

"You have that kind of curiosity about someone who could be there to kill you?"

"Sure," I said. "I'm a foolish man. You know that."

"Watch your mouth, feller."

I grinned at him so hard that the scar across my back got tight. "Go to hell!"

"Listen . . ."

"No, you listen, you stinking, miserable little slob . . . don't tell me to watch my mouth. Don't tell me one lousy little thing to do at all or I'll tell you where to shove it. Don't try to peg me because I have a record. . . ."

In back of me the tall boy stopped smiling and hissed, "Let him say it out."

"Damn right, let me say it out. You got no choice. You're not fooling with a parolee or a hooker who's scared stiff of cops. I hate cops in general and right now you slobs in particular. This little shake has all the earmarks of a frame and brother, you're going in over your head if you try it."

"That all?"

"No," I said. "Now I'm done playing. I went along for the ride to see what the bit was and it stinks. So I leave. If you think I can't, then put the arm on me and try stopping me. Then you monkeys are going to have a pretty time trying to explain this setup to a couple of tabloids I got friends on."

The thin one said, "Finished?"

"Yeah. Now I'm leaving."

"Don't go."

I stopped and stared at him. Nobody had moved to get in my way at all. There was something tight about the way they all stood there, something all wrong about the play that I couldn't make. I could feel my back going tight again and I said, "What?"

The thin one swung around in his chair. "I thought you said you were a curious person."

I went back to the table. "Okay, friend. But before I get suckered in, answer me some questions."

The thin one nodded, his face impassive.

"You're cops."

He nodded, but now there was something new in his eyes. "All right, I'll qualify it. We're cops . . . of a sort."

I asked, "Who am I?"

His answer was flat and methodical. "Ryan. The Irish One. Sixteen arrests, one conviction for assault and battery. Suspected of being involved in several killings, several robberies and an uncooperative witness in three homicide cases. Associates with known criminals, has no visible source of income except for partial disability pension from World War II. Present address . . ."

"That's enough," I said.

He paused and leaned back. "Also—you're rather astute."

"Thanks. I went to college for two years."

"It made a difference criminally?"

"It made no difference one way or another. Get on with the pitch."

His fingers made a slow roll on the table top.

"You knew you had been tailed for two weeks. Do you know why?"

"First guess is that you're figuring a fix for me to turn stoolie," I said. "If that's it you've wasted time because you aren't that smart to catch me off base."

"Then you think you're smarter than an entire law enforcement agency?"

They watched me. Nobody said a thing.

Finally I said, "Okay. I'm a curious guy. Spell it out slow in punk language so I won't miss the juicy parts."

The others left the room when the thin one nodded.

He said, "There is a job that must be done. We can't do it because of several factors involved. One is simple enough to understand; it is possible . . . even probable that we are known to those of . . . the opposition forces. The other reason has a psychological factor involved."

"It must be a beauty," I said.

He went on as if he had never heard me. "Our groups are highly skilled. Although those chosen to augment our group are of the finest calibre, the most select, elite . . . they still have certain handicaps civilized society has inflicted on them. Maybe you can finish it for me."

I nodded. "Sure. Let's try a lucky guess. You need an animal. Some improver of the breed has run all shagginess out of your business-suit characters and you need a downtown shill to bait your hook. How close did I come?"

"Close," he said.

"I'm still listening."

"We need somebody of known talents. Like you. Somebody whose mind can deal on an exact level with . . . the opposition. We need someone whose criminal disposition can be directed into certain channels."

"An animal," I said, "the dirty kind. Maybe a jackal that can play around in the jungle with the big ones without being caught."

"It's descriptive enough."

"Not quite. The rest of it is that if he's killed he wouldn't even be missed or counted for a loss."

When he answered, he said, "That isn't exactly *'punk language'*."

"But I'm there, huh?"

"You're there," he said solemnly.

I shook my head slowly. *"Brother!"* I pushed away from the desk and straightened up. "I think you made a mistake in nomenclature, buddy. It's not a psychological factor involved, it's a philosophical one. Only your appeal is psychological. You posed me a pretty, laddie."

"I . . . don't suppose it would do much good to appeal on a patriotic basis?"

"You suppose right. You can shove flag-waving and duty-to-your country crap with the rest of it."

"Then how do I appeal?"

"To curiosity and one thing more. Money"

"How much?"

I grinned real big, all the way across my face. "A bundle, friend. For what you want, a bundle. Tax-free, no strings, in small, used bills."

"What is it that I wanted?" he asked.

For fun I played it straight. I said, "You clued me, friend. Patriotism doesn't exist on any local level. Suddenly we're international and I can only think of three fields where you striped pantsers could exploit me. The narcotic trade through Italy, Mexico or China; illegal gold shipments to Europe; then last, the Commies."

He didn't answer.

"How much?" I asked.

"You can get your bundle."

"Like I said? Tax free, small bills . . ."

"Like you said," he repeated.

"One more point."

"Ask it," he told me.

"What makes you think I'll like the bit?"

"Because you hate cops and politicians and those are the kind of people you'll get a chance to really crack down on."

I squinted at him. "You're leaving something out."

"You're right, Irish. You're communicating now, boy. I left out the needle. Money is a powerful motivator, but the needle still has to be there. If you take the deal we supply the *toxin-anti-toxin*."

"So?"

"You'll take it?"

I nodded. "Sure. What'd you expect me to say?"

"Nothing." With his fingers he drew a paper from his

pocket, unfolded it so the bottom showed with the signature line and nothing more, then he passed me his pen. "Sign it."

The laugh came out of me of its own accord. Why ask to read it? I had nothing I could sign away and nothing to confess to that couldn't be broken in court and nothing makes me more curious than signing first and asking to read later. I signed.

I said, "What's the pitch?"

"Nothing you'd appreciate. To protect ourselves or yourself under impossibly remote circumstances you now have a certain measure of legal protection."

"Like what?"

"Like you were just made a cop," he said.

I took it easy and said all the words slowly and plainly so he wouldn't miss a one and after a long time I ran out. His face had turned white and the corners of his mouth were pulled back tight.

"You finished?" he said.

"It's all the punk language I can think of right now."

"I don't like the arrangement any better than you do. It's a necessity or it never would have happened. You're in."

"Suppose I crap out?"

"You won't."

"Okay, I asked for it. Now what do you do, indoctrinate me or something?"

"Not at all. All you're going to do is be given a name. You'll find that person. Then whatever is necessary to do . . . you do."

"Damn, man, can't you make sense?"

The smile came back again. "Making sense of it is your job. The picture will come clear by itself. You'll know what to do."

"Sure. Great." I asked the question. "Who?"

"The name is Lodo."

"That's all?"

He nodded. "That's all. Just find him. You'll know what to do."

"Then the loot?"

"A big bundle of it. More than you've ever had in your life."

"How long do I have?"

"No time limit."

I let the laugh out easily. His eyes tightened when the laugh spread to my face. "Just for the record before we turn the machine off, friend . . . who steered you to me?"

"A man named Billings. Henry Billings. Familiar?"

Something choked the laugh off in my throat. "Yeah, I know him."

Know him? The lousy slob ratted on me to the M.P.'s about liberating 10 grand of some kraut's gold hoard back in '45 and while I was getting the guardhouse treatment when some planted coins were found in my footlocker, he walked off with the stuff himself. The day I caught up with him would be his last.

When I knew nothing was showing on my face I said, "Where could I find him?"

"Out in Brooklyn . . . in a cemetery."

I felt like kicking the walls out of the building. I had nursed that hate for too long to have it snatched away from me like that. *Twenty years now I had been waiting.*

"What happened?"

"He was shot."

"Yeah?"

"He was after the same name."

I said, "Yeah?" again.

"Before he died he recommended you. He said you were the only one he knew who was a bigger bastard than he was himself."

"He was lying."

"You still with it?"

"Sure." *I wouldn't miss it for anything now. Someplace Billings had bought something with that 10 G's and whatever he got was mine now no matter who I had to take it away from.* "Where do I start?"

"With a phone number. Billings had it on him."

"Whose?" I said.

"You find out. We couldn't figure it."

Once again he dipped into his pocket. He came up with a pad and wrote a phone number on it, a Murray Hill exchange. He let me see it, then tore it out and held a match under it.

Outside, I whistled up a cab and cruised back toward the main stem, trying hard to think my way out of the situation. It had all the earmarks of a sucker trap and somehow I got elected to try it out. Me, strictly Brooklyn Irish, old Ryan himself, heading straight for the plastic pottie boobie prize.

Man, I thought, I'm not new to this business. I've been around a long while and made plenty the easy way without pulling time. Even the hard boys on the big team uptown stayed off my back.

At 49th St. and Sixth Ave. I paid off the cabbie and walked to Joe DiNuccio's. I went into the back room where I knew Art Shay would be and slid in across the booth from him.

Art's a funny guy. He does feature writing for a syndicated outfit, but he could have been a great reporter or TV analyst if something hadn't happened between him and some broad before he got back from Germany in '45. Now he was spending all his time on assignments, working hard to get himself killed.

His eyes peered at me over the top of the galley proofs he was checking. "What're you crawling after now?"

I grinned at him. "Something funny's happening to me."

"That shouldn't be a new feeling for you, Ryan. Who's bump list you on now?"

"Art," I said. "Tell me something. Have you ever known the fuzz to use a hood for anything except a stoolie?"

The corners of his eyes stretched taut. "No. Not the straight boys, anyway. What have you got going?"

"Nothing special. I'm just curious about a few things."

"Any story in it?"

"Maybe."

"Want to talk about it?"

"Not yet. Things aren't squared away. Maybe you can fit in some pieces. Ever hear of a man named Billings?"

His eyes opened a little wider. "Same one who got gunned down a few days ago?"

I nodded.

"It was just a squib in the paper. Called a gang killing." He stopped suddenly and looked at me hard. "Ryan . . . I remember ten years back when you were talking about killing a guy by that name. Did you tap him?"

"I didn't have the luck, kiddo. That tap was somebody else's."

"The conversation is fascinating, Ryan. Keep it up."

"Okay, read this. Billings wasn't a small tap at all. That guy had something so big it would have made front page for a week."

"Like what?"

I shook my head. "I'm new to it too."

"How are you involved?"

"Because Billings had something he knew could get me killed too. It was the last thing he ever did, but he did it good. That warped slob had to live like a snake just to stay alive ever since he framed me and he made up for it, all right." I stopped and grinned real big. "At least he thought he did."

Art dropped his chin in his hand and nodded. "What can I do?"

"As an accredited reporter, you can get some official answers. Get any statement Billings made and any details on how he was killed. Can do?"

"Shouldn't be hard. Those reports are on file." He waited a moment, then said, "You're giving me a small worm for a big hook."

"Thanks." I uncurled myself and got up. "Ever know anyone called Lodo?"

He thought a moment, then shook his head. "Nothing there. Important?"

"Who knows. Think on it."

"Sure. Where can I reach you?"

"Remember Papa Manny's old three-floor brownstone?"

"Off Second?"

"I own it now. I live in the basement apartment."

The Murray Hill exchange the thin one had given me wasn't a phone. It was a coded password that got you admission into a horse parlor operating right on Broadway. It wasn't one of the things the cops could be expected to know, not even the grafters.

But I knew. I even had the latest job. The one they gave me was three weeks old. The boy on the door winked, said, "Hi, Ryan, come in an' spend a buck."

The place had changed some. The loot was flowing in. The board was bigger, there was free booze at a service bar and fat chairs where the benches used to be.

Jake McGaffney came out from behind the pay window, saw me and came over. "Changing rackets, kid?"

"Not me, Jake. I like mine better. They got to be sure things for me."

"We got a few of those too," he chuckled. "What's on your mind?"

I nudged his arm and steered him to the end of the pay window. "You getting touched by anybody?"

"You know this operation, Ryan. We're not paying off. Hell, the cops know we're operating, but we move too fast for them to line us up."

"Nobody trying to cut in?"

"Get with it, boy. Since I played ball at the trial, uptown lets me go my own way. Sure, they give me limits and it's okay with me. Nobody's shaking me though. What's got you?"

"Did you know Billings?"

"Sure. He got gunned." Then he stopped and his face looked drawn. "He didn't leave any tracks to this place, did he?"

"Nothing that can tie in. The fuzz had an old MU code he wrote down."

Jake let his face relax and picked a butt from his pack and lit it. Through the smoke he said, "I'm okay then. They would've hit me before this if they figured it."

"Jake . . . got any idea why Billings got tapped?"

"Idea?" He laughed in his chest. "Hell, man, I *know why.*"

"Why, Jake?"

"He had twelve thousand skins in his pocket when he left here. A nag called *Annie's Foot* came in and he was riding it hard."

"He been coming here long?"

"A month, maybe. I got a memo on him from his first play if you want it."

"Who steered him in?"

"Gonzales. You know little Juan Gonzales . . . he's the one pulled that kid outa the Hudson River sometime back and got his picture in the tabs. He was down the docks goofing off when this lady starts to scream and . . ."

"Where is he now, Jake?"

"Gonzales?" he seemed surprised. "He got killed three weeks ago. He got loaded and stepped right out in front of a truck. He got dead quick. No waiting around."

I said, "He have a family?"

"Just some dame. You wait. . . . I'll get you the business."

He went behind the window and poked around in a card file until he found what he wanted. It was a short history of Juan Gonzales and when I memorized the data I handed it back. "Keep it if you want," he said.

"I don't need it."

Juan Gonzales had lived on 54th, a few houses down from Tenth Ave. It was a fringe area where total integration of the underprivileged of all classes fused into a hotbed of constant violence. Lucinda Gonzales had a second floor rear apartment. The bells never worked in these tenements so I just went up and knocked at the door. It opened on a chain and a pretty, dark face peered at me and queried, "Si . . . who is it?"

"Lucinda Gonzales?"

"Si."

"I want to speak about Juan. Can I come in?"

She hesitated, shrugged, then closed the door to unhook the chain. I stepped inside and she leaned back against the door.

"I can tell you are not the policeman."

"That's right."

"You are not one of Juan's friends, either."

"How do you know?"

"His friends are all peegs. Not even tough guys. Just peegs."

"Thanks."

"What you want?"

"I want to know about Juan. You married?" ·

She made a wry face. "Nothing by the church. But this is not what you want to say."

This time I gave her a little grin. "Okay, chicken . . . I'll put it this way . . . Juan got loaded and got himself killed. He . . ."

"He did?" the sarcasm was thick. I stopped and let her say the rest. "Juan did not drink, señor."

"What's bothering you, Lucinda?"

"You, señor." Her arms were folded tightly across her breasts, making them half rise from her dress. "To me you look like the one who could do it."

"Do what?"

"Make Juan go crazy with fear. Maybe chase him so he runs in front of the truck and gets killed. All this time I have waited because I knew soon that somebody would come. They would have to come here. There is no other place. Now you are here, señor, and I can kill you like I have been waiting to do."

She unfolded her arms. In one hand she had a snub-nose rod and at that distance there wasn't a chance she could miss me.

"You better be sure, chicken," I said.

Her voice was getting a hysterical calm. There was a dull happy look in her eyes that meant she was crowding the deep end and so was I. "I *am* sure, señor."

I said very deliberately, "How do you know?"

"I know those of who Juan would be afraid. You are such a one. You thought he had his money when he died. He did not. Those ten thousand dollars, señor . . . it was here."

"Ten thousand . . ." My voice was soft, but she heard it.

Her smile was vicious. "But it is not here now. It is safe. It is in the bank and it is mine. For such a sum Juàn died. Now you can follow him."

She took too long to shoot. She thought of Juan first and her eyes flooded at the wrong time. I slapped my hand over hers and the firing pin bit into my skin when I yanked the rod out of her hand. When she started to scream, I belted her across the mouth and knocked her into a chair. She tried another one and I backhanded it loose and as though I snapped my fingers, the glazed look left her eyes and she stared at me from a face contorted by fear.

When she had it long enough I said, "Ease off. You won't get hurt."

She didn't believe me. She had lived with one idea too long.

"Lucinda . . . I never knew Juan. I don't want his bundle. That clear?"

She nodded.

"Where'd the ten grand come from?"

Defiance showed across her face. Then it all came back again; fear, disbelief, hatred, defiance.

I said, "Listen to me, sugar. If I wanted to I could make you talk a real easy way. It wouldn't be hard. I could make you scream and talk and scream and talk and you couldn't stop it. You know this?"

She bobbed her head once, quickly.

"But I don't want anything that bad. I'm not going to do anything like that. Understand?"

"Si."

"Then once more . . . where'd the ten G's come from?"

Nervously, she ran her fingers through her hair. "He came home from the docks one day and told me that soon we would go back to the island. Only now it would not be a mud hut but in a fine building that we would live. He said we were going to have much money. We would travel around the world, maybe."

"When was this?"

"The week before he died, señor."

"He had it then?"

"No." She stood up quickly and stepped to the table, turned and leaned back against it. "He was *getting* it then, he said. He was feeling very good. But he did not drink."

She shrugged. "He changed. He became a scared one. He would tell me nothing. Nothing at all. The same night he . . . died . . ." she paused and put her face in her hands a moment before going on, " . . . he came in and took something from where he hid it in the closet."

"What was it?"

"I do not know. It was not very big. I theenk it could have been a gun. One time he kept a gun there wrapped up in rags. He did not show me. He went out for maybe an hour. When he came back he had this money. He gave it to me and told me to pack up. Then he left."

"Where to?"

"To die somewhere, señor. He said he was going to . . . how you say it . . . arrange things."

"You have the dough."

"Is it really mine?"

I flipped the rod in my hand then tossed it on top of the table. "Sure it's yours," I told her. "Why not?"

She picked up the gun, studied it and laid it down again. "I am sorry if I . . . almost shot you."

"You could have been sorrier. You could have gotten your picture in the morning papers real easy."

Her smile was grim. "Yes. Like Juan." She opened a drawer in the dish closet and took out two front pages from recent tabloids and handed them to me. In one Juan was a hero. In the other he was dead.

But on his last public appearance there was an out-of-character bit for what I had been thinking. The truck driver who killed him was sitting on the curb crying.

I reached for the door. Before I opened it I said, "Did Juan ever mention a man named Lodo?"

"Lodo? Si. Twice he says this name. It was when he was very scared."

I let go the door, all edgy again. "Who is he?"

"He was asleep when he said this name, señor. I do not know. I do not ask, either."

I closed the door quietly behind me and went back downstairs.

It had started to rain and the street stank.

The truck that had killed Juan was one of the Abart fleet from Brooklyn. I told the harried little boss I was an insurance investigator and he told me I had 20 minutes before Harry Peeler would be in and to have a seat.

At 5:40 a short thin guy with grey hair came in and the girl there said, "That gentleman's waiting to see you, Harry. Insurance investigator."

"It's about the . . . accident, I suppose."

"Well, yes."

"Terrible." He glanced at me ruefully. "I'm finished driving, Mr. Ryan. I can't go it any more."

"I want you to tell me about that night."

"But I told . . ."

"You've had a chance to think it over since then, Mr. Peeler. You've gone over every detail a thousand times, haven't you?"

He moaned, "Oh, help me, yes. Yes, every night. I can't forget it."

"Tell me about it, Mr. Peeler."

"How can I explain something crazy like that? It was three A.M. and nobody was on the streets. I was driving toward the bridge when this guy comes from in front of this parked truck. Right under the wheels!"

"Was he running?"

At first he didn't answer. When he looked up, he had a puzzled expression working at his face, then he said, "He kind of flew."

"What?"

"I know it sounds crazy, but that's what it was like. He must have been standing there all along, just waiting. He didn't run. He dove, like. You know what I mean. Maybe he was committing suicide. He dove, like."

"Could he have been pushed, like?"

Harry Peeler's eyes opened wide, startled. He swallowed hard, thinking. "He . . . could have been."

"You've been thinking that, haven't you?"

He swallowed again.

I said, "It wasn't your fault. You couldn't have done anything to prevent it."

He wasn't looking at me. He was squinting at the far wall and I heard him say, "Somebody ran from behind that truck. I know it. It took a while to remember, but I know it! I was yelling for somebody to get a doctor. It was a long while before anybody came. Somebody was behind that truck, though."

I stood up and patted his shoulder. "Okay. You feel better now?"

"Sure." He grinned. "It ain't good to kill somebody, but it's better knowing you couldn't of stopped it anyhow."

"That's the way. You keep driving."

I made a double check around Harry Peeler's neighborhood. He was a long time resident and strictly a family man. Everybody liked the guy. When I got done asking questions, I was pretty sure of one thing.

Harry Peeler hadn't been in on any killing except by coincidence.

The rain had started again, driving the city indoors. DiNuccio's was crowded and smelled of beer and damp clothes. Art was waiting for me, in the back. When I sat down, I said, "Let's have it."

"Sure. Killed with a .38 slug in the chest, two in the stomach. Now here's an item the papers didn't have. He wasn't shot where he died. My guess is that he was thrown from a car. The officers on the scene first aren't talking so it's my guess again that he talked before he kicked off. Item two: I ran into so many icy stares when I pushed this thing that I got the idea something pretty hot was being covered up. A check through a good friend came up with this bit . . . there's some kind of a grumble on where the high hoods sit."

"What else on Billings?"

"Briefly, his last address was a midtown hotel and the name a phony. He was traced back through two others, but no further."

"Source of income?"

"His latest room had an assortment of bum dice and new-but-marked decks of cards very cleverly packaged and stamped. He was a sharpie. A few receipted bills and match covers placed him working cheap places around here and in Jersey."

"Ten years," I said. "All that time under my nose and I never got near him."

"Be happy, chum." He flipped his pages over and scanned them, picking out pieces of information. "One thing more. I found a couple of shills he played with before he died. He was talking about having a roll waiting. He was going into big time. Nobody paid any attention to him right then."

I thought a moment, remembering how Billings operated in the army. "Was he flush when he played?"

"Those shills said he always had enough risk capital to entice some nice fat bankrolls." He looked at me and put his notes away. "Now let's hear what you have to say," he said softly.

I shook my head at him. "This is stupid. Everything's

doubling back. It starts and ends too fast. You sure you got everything on Billings?"

"Yeah." I waved the waiter over for a beer and then knocked half of it off in a long pull. "I'm going to guess a little bit here, but see how it works out.

"Billings was a funny guy. He used to say he'd wait for the big one to come along if he waited all his life. He foxed me out of ten grand in the army and when I got out of the guardhouse, he'd been discharged. He hung onto that roll and used it as sucker bait for his rigged games. I doubt if he took anybody for too much. That would have spoiled it. Those games were listening posts waiting for that big one. All he'd bother to make would be living expenses.

"Then a guy named Juan Gonzales, who was a small time pay-off man for a friend of mine, must have sat in, saw the roll and talked up horses. He even got Billings passed into the rooms. Matter of fact, the night he was killed he had twelve G's on him."

Art let out a slow whistle. "He was clean when he was found."

"Nobody would let that lay around, kiddo. It could have been a motive for his death."

"For twelve G's he could get a firstclass ride in this town, not just a plain mugging."

I said, "Now listen . . . this Juan Gonzales had been killed a couple weeks earlier. Before he got it he was talking big money to his common-law wife, then he got scared spitless for some reason, showed up with ten grand, handed it to her and went out and got bumped."

"I remember the case. Front page. He had just . . ."

"That's the guy."

"In other words, your point is that in either case the motive could possibly be robbery."

"Yeah, only it isn't. First because I'm in and next because there's a lid on the deal. It's real stupid. Everything doubles back. You sure you have everything on Billings?"

"He was buried at the city's expense and the only bunch of flowers came from the *Lazy Dazy Flower Shop*. The graveyard attendant remembered the name. If you want him exhumed, dig him up yourself."

"Sure." I threw a buck on the table. "Keep in touch."

My watch said 9:55 and I was tired. I found a cab outside, got off at my corner and started up toward my apartment.

The first pitch came from Pete-the-Dog who sold papers with a broken-throated growl. It came again from Mamie Huggins who waited until I passed by to put out her garbage and it came again by low whistle from the shadows across the street.

Two of them. Unknowns. They were waiting in my apartment.

I came through the back way Papa Manny always used when the police raided the old love factory he ran. I picked up the .45 from the shelf, cocked it under my arm so the click of the hammer was inaudible and stood there in the dark until my eyes were used to it.

One stood looking out the window. The other sat right in front of me and he was the one I put the cold snout of the gun against. I said, "Be at ease, laddies. You move and you're dead."

I stepped inside and prodded my boy. He got up obediently and walked to the wall. The other one got the idea and did the same. They both leaned against it while I patted them down and waited while I flicked on the light. Then I dumped the shells from the *Cobras* they carried in belt holsters and laid them on an end table. They both were too mad to spit.

The guy from the window I knew. I had met him a few days ago up in that apartment far above the city. The other was a new face. That one looked at me coldly, then to the gun. "You have a license for that?"

I grinned at him. "Let's say a poetic one, cop. I signed a piece of paper up there the boss man says allows me certain liberties."

"There's only one copy and it can be torn up very easily."

"Not for a simple fracture like this, you slob. Now knock it off. If you're so damn dumb you can't break and enter without being spotted you ought to join the fire department."

The other one said, "Lay off, Ryan."

"Okay," I said. "So let's hear what's going on and get out."

He hated me silently and then put on his blank face again. "To be simple about it, we'd like a progress report."

I said, "Nobody told me anything about this junket. I got sent off cold. What do you expect from me?"

"All right. What do you want to know?"

"How did you contact Billings?"

"We didn't. He came to us. He had something to sell."

"Like what?"

"We don't know. It was international in scope and big enough to cause a muss in this country. Our people overseas picked up information that there was trouble in high places. It was from there that we found out that Billings was a key figure."

"Somebody has quite an organization," I said.

"It's as big as ours."

"Go on."

"Billings apparently overplayed it. He wanted to sell what he had. We decided to go along. We assigned four men to keep him protected . . . top men, I might add. They worked in teams of two and both teams were killed. Four good men, Ryan, highly trained, killed like rank amateurs. It was Billings who found the last team. He called and said he was getting out and that was when he told us about you."

"He got out, all right. He was as cute as you with a trick dodge. He didn't last very long, though. He caught it that night."

"Nothing was in the paper about those boys getting killed."

"That was easy enough to fix."

"Yeah." I walked across the room and pulled a cold beer from the cooler. "Tell me . . . Billings wasn't dead when he was found. What did he say?"

I watched their faces. They couldn't help it, but their eyes touched, briefly.

"Okay, Ryan, you're sharp. He wasn't dead. He said it was Lodo. That's where we got the name. We have nothing else on it."

They didn't know and I didn't tell them that another dead man had known Lodo. How many more?

I said, "One more thing . . . was any money found on Billings?"

His voice was a little too flat. "What do you mean?"

"The police reports say he was clean. It earmarked a robbery."

"So?"

"What happened to the twelve grand?"

My friend held his mouth tight. "How did you know about that?"

"I get around."

Before he could answer, it came to me. It was all backwards and wrong, but it could make sense to them. I said, "If you're thinking I sold him something for twelve grand, you're gone, man. You just loused your picture up. Now I'm reading you R5-S5. You pigs conned me into taking on a kill job with hopes of hanging me. All this while I had in the back of my mind I was doing something that could make you idiots look jerky and because you asked me to at that. In fact, a couple of times I caught myself enjoying doing something straight for a change. Brother, what a sucker I was!

"So my old buddy Billings tips you to me before he's found dead with twelve G's in his pocket. So I'm on the spot. Oh, man, this is crazy. What was I supposed to do . . . get so shook that I left a hole in my scheme somewhere that I'd try backtracking until I tripped myself up?"

I let go of the mad slowly, and when I had it down where it belonged, I grinned at them. "Laddies, you're devious thinkers, but you thunk wrong. I got you by the short hairs now. I'm in and you're out. I'm going to ride this one for all it's worth. I'm so far ahead of you right now it's pathetic and it'll stay that way. You tell the boss man to get that pile of small bills ready, y'hear?"

They didn't answer me.

"I want one more thing," I said. "I want a copy of my 'appointment' and a number where you guys can be reached sent to me care of General Delivery at 34th Street. I want a license for this gun and the number is 127569. Remember it. Now blow out of here and don't bother laying a tail on me. It won't work. If I want you I'll call and that's the only progress report you'll get."

You go up 16 floors and you get off in a plush foyer surrounded by antique furniture and a lovely redhead who smiles and you are encompassed by *Peter F. Haynes, III, Co., Inc.*

She looked up at me, button by button until she came to my eyes, then she stopped and smiled a little bit bigger. To her I was something different than the usual Haynes client even though mine was a $200 suit. The shirt was white and the collar spread. The tie was black knitted and neat and the cuffs that showed were the proper half inch below the coat cuff. The links were plain, but gold, and they showed. The only thing out of place was my face. I don't think I looked like the typical Haynes client. I wasn't carrying a briefcase, either. I was carrying a rod, but that was one reason for the $200 suit. It didn't show.

The redhead said, "Good morning."

I said, "Hello, honey."

She said, "Can I help you?"

I said, "Anytime."

She said, "Please . . ."

I said, "I should be the one to say please."

She said, "*Stop* it!"

I said, "What'll you give me if I do?"

Then she smiled and said, "You're crazy."

I smiled back, "Is Carmen Smith here?"

"It would have to be her," she said. "Yes, she's here. Is she expecting you?"

"No."

"Then you can't see her."

"Who's going to keep me out?" I said.

She got the grin back. "Nobody around here, I guess. Miss Smith is down the hall, at the end. She'll be mad."

"Tough."

She went down the buttons again in reverse. "I hope so. Stop by to say so-long."

I grinned at her. "I will, don't worry."

Miss Smith was encompassed by two girl secretaries and a queer. She was behind a desk talking into a hush-a-phone, doodling on an early *Times* edition. When I walked in, I waved a thumb at the dolls and they got out. The queer took longer until he looked straight at me. Miss Smith said something into the HP and hung up. Then she pushed back her chair and stood up.

Most times a woman is nothing. Sometimes you can classify them as pretty or not pretty. Sometimes you can say this one I like or this one I do not like.

Then one day you see one who is totally unlike all the rest and this is one you not only like but one you must have. This is one who has been waiting a long time for somebody and instinctively you know that until now she hasn't found that one. She's big and beautiful and stands square-shouldered like a man, but she's full-breasted and taut and completely undressed beneath the sheath she has on. She's not trying for anything. She doesn't have to. You don't have to look to know she's long-legged and round and in her loins there's a subtle fire that can be fanned, and fanned, and fanned.

I said the obvious. "Miss Smith?"

"Yes."

"My name is Ryan."

"I have no morning appointments."

"Now you have, kitten."

I let her take a good look at me. It didn't take long.

She knew. I wasn't taking any apple out of her hand.

"Can I help you?"

"Sure, honey. That you can do."

"Well."

"A flower shop . . . the Lazy Dazy . . . in Brooklyn, tells me you sent a bouquet to a friend of mine."

It would be hard to describe the brief play that went across her face.

"Billings," I said. "He was killed. He got one bunch of flowers. Yours."

Again, it happened, that sympathetic sweep of emotions touching her eyes and her mouth. She sat down at an angle, woman-like, with her knees touching, and her hand on the desk shook a little.

"You . . . are a friend?"

"Not of his. Were you?"

Her eyes filled up and she made a motion with her head before reaching for the tissues in her drawer. "I'm sorry. I can never quite get used to people dying whom I know."

"Don't let it get you, sugar. He wasn't worth it."

"I know, but he was still someone I was familiar with. May I ask who you are?"

"The name is Ryan, honey. In common parlance I'm a hood. Not a big one, but I get along."

There was a silent appeal in her eyes. "I don't . . . quite . . ."

"Where do you come off knowing a bummer like Billings?"

"Why should I tell you?"

"Because if I don't get the answer, the cops will."

She sucked in her breath, filling the tanned skin of her bosom, swelling it against the dress.

I said, "How well did you know Billings?"

"Tell me something first. Since you seem so interested in me, have you . . . let's say . . . investigated me in any way?"

"Nope."

"Mr. Ryan . . . I'm a gambler."

"A good one?"

"One of the best. My father was a professional. According to his need or current morals, he would work it right or wrong. No better card mechanic ever lived. He supported me in style."

"You . . . ?"

"Mother died at my birth. My father never married

again. He gave me everything including an education in mechanics to the point where I can clean a table any time I want to."

"This doesn't explain Billings."

"I'm a card player, Mr. Ryan. I'm in on all the big games that ever happen in this city. I win more than I could possibly make at a mundane job from fat little men who love to show off before a woman. If you're really a hood, then ask around the slap circuit who I am. I'm sure they'll be able to tell you."

"I don't have to ask. But that still doesn't explain Billings."

"Billings was a queer draw. He was a good mechanic at times, but not good enough to work against the big ones. Straight, he was all right. One day he sat in with us and I caught him working and cut him loose. He never did figure it until I got him invited again. You see, Mr. Ryan, these types are fun for me. I was able to chop him down to nothing just for the fun of it."

"How much did you take him for?"

"Just for hundreds. He had money, but we were playing for cards, understand? Money isn't quite that important."

"He was good?"

"Very. But just not that good."

"When did you see him last?"

She didn't hesitate. "Three days before he was killed."

"This you can prove?"

When she had her composure back, she said simply, "I should never have sent him flowers."

"That wasn't the bit, kid."

"No? What was then?"

"You're a big gal. A VP of a promising industry. You make fifteen hundred a week in your job and while the boss is away you're head doll here. You have a penthouse on Madison Avenue and charge accounts in the best stores. So you like to gamble. You like to play cards. This wasn't hard to find out at all."

"I thought you hadn't investigated me."

"I didn't. I picked it all up from one talkative building attendant."

"Then why are you considering me suspect, Mr. Ryan?" The tears were there.

"You sent him a five-dollar bouquet, kid."

And she didn't hesitate this time, either. "He was a five-dollar card player, Mr. Ryan."

"And you're sentimental?"

"No, but it was a gesture to the cheap dead."

"The gesture could be vindictive."

"When you're dead it doesn't matter. It was a gesture. Now I'm sorry for it."

"I don't like it, baby," I told her softly.

When she looked up, the VP was gone and I could have been looking at her across a table somewhere. She was all woman and coldly wild, with full-house eyes ready to sweat me out. It only lasted a second, but while it did I knew there was no bluff.

She said, "My father was well known at Monte Carlo. He was even better known at Vegas. His name wasn't Smith. One day he was shot by a crazy little man who lost his own roll with his own marked cards."

"What happened to the crazy little man?"

"The nine-year-old daughter of the dead man blew his head off with a shotgun from ten feet away."

I said quietly, "You?"

"Me."

"You sent *him* a five-dollar bouquet too?"

"No." Her smile was clean and straight across. "The girl daddy was living with did, though."

"I like the gesture," I said coldly.

"I think it was fitting." Her tone matched mine.

"Now?"

"Something has come up as regards Mr. Billings. He was killed and now you're here. Not the police. Just you. Why?"

I said, "Billings left me to the dogs for ten grand one time. I think he did it again. I'm a little anxious to find out who's involved in this play."

"You think I might be one?"

"I don't know, but baby . . . I'm going to find out real soon."

"I'm not sorry he's dead," she said. "To me it doesn't matter one way or another. In a way, perhaps, I'm glad, nevertheless, I don't care. How you fit into this is no concern of mine. Is there anything else?"

I grinned and stood up and leaned over her desk. I said, "Yeah, kid, one thing more. Like you've been told a million times, you're an interesting wench. I wish you weren't out of it. From now on it's all going to be real dull."

Until now she hadn't smiled. When she did it was with a wet mouth and white teeth that made something happen no matter how early it was. She was hazel eyes, and suddenly chestnut hair, then even more quickly something slippery your hands should try to hold but couldn't.

She was big. Not as big as me, but big. When she uncurled and faced me she said, "No . . . I'll have to change it for you. Nobody ever called me that before."

"What before?"

"Merely interesting."

"My apologies."

"Not accepted here, Mr. Ryan." She looked at her watch, then smiled across at me. "It's almost noon. I'll let you apologize at lunch."

"It's getting cute again, kid."

Her smile had a question in it, then she understood what I meant. She laughed outright this time. "Let me put it this way, Mr. Ryan . . . there is a reason I want to be with you a little longer. You see, I've known many men . . . but I never had lunch with a real hood before. Shall we go?"

I took her to Pat Shane's for lunch. We ate on the dark side, in a back booth away from big ears and cigar smoke. By the time the steaks were gone, there was little I didn't know about Carmen Smith.

She reached across the table and laid her hand on top of mine. "Ryan . . . do you think you'll ever find out who killed Billings?"

I turned my hand over and held hers. "I'll find them."

"Is it . . . dangerous?"

That got a short laugh from me. "It's not exactly a soft touch. A couple of guys already died."

"A couple?"

"Just a detail. A little guy named Juan Gonzales. Ever hear of him?"

"No . . . it isn't familiar."

A second thought occurred to me. "Look, Carmen . . . when Billings was around you . . . was he ever scared?"

"The last time he was . . . well, nervous. He played pretty badly."

"Were the stakes big?"

"Very petty that time. We all kidded him about it. He didn't say anything."

"Tell me . . . did he ever mention the name Lodo to you at all?"

"Lodo?" She paused, then shook her head. "No, not Billings. But I've heard it somewhere. Who is he?"

"I don't know . . . yet. I'll find out, though."

This time she took my hand in both of hers. "Please be careful, Ryan."

"Sure, but why, kitten?"

"I might want to have lunch with a big hood again." She took her hand away with a smile, looked at her watch and reached for her pocketbook. "Time to leave. I'll make a quick visit first."

"Go ahead. I'll meet you up front."

Eddie Mack and Fats Sebull, a pair of guys I know, were talking to Pat and saw me coming. Fats said, "Pretty company you got."

"Great. She okay, Fats?"

"We had her checked. She's okay. One hell of a card player, though."

"That's what I hear."

Eddie Mack asked me, "How'd you meet her?"

"Checking on Billings."

He snorted. "Him. He won't be missed." He stopped, looked at me with a frown. "You knew him?"

"I wanted to kill him, buddy. I got beat out."

He glanced around him nervously and licked his lips. "Say, Ryan . . . you got any idea who tapped him?"

"An idea. A guy named Lodo. You ever hear of him?"

It was Pat's face that rang the bell. His eyes had a funny look and something had happened to the set of his mouth.

I said, "Pat?"

He motioned with his hand to keep it quiet. "Man, that's a trouble name."

"You know him?"

"I don't want to, kid, but a couple days ago `two scared union representatives were in here and one made a phone call from the booths in back when I was in the office. He didn't know I was there, but I could hear him. When I bothered to listen, he was saying that there were some marked boys around and that Lodo had showed up. Apparently he had picked it up accidentally and he told the other guy he was clearing out."

"That was all?"

"Enough for me, friend. Any bumping I don't want done on the premises. I don't even want people around who know about them things. I've had all that crap I want."

"Don't get so shook, Patsy boy."

"Look, Ryan, if you're in this, then keep it someplace else."

I grinned and nodded.

Behind them Carmen was walking toward me and everybody in the place was watching her. She said, "Hello, Fats . . . Eddie. You know Ryan?"

Fats said, "We've met."

I nodded to them and walked out with her. We got into a cab.

"Taking me to be verified by Fats and Eddie was smart. Are you satisfied?"

I looked at her and grinned. "Not satisfied at all, kitten."

Her smile came back fast. She reached over with her hand and pulled my head toward hers and suddenly there was a fire on my mouth that was alive and wet and a little shocking.

When she stopped it was too soon and she said, "I never kissed a hood before, either." She touched my mouth with a finger. "Satisfied now?"

"No," I said, and I grinned.

"You're cool, big boy, real big and ugly and cool, man."

"That's not VP talk, sugar."

"I thought maybe you'd understand it better," she mocked.

"Talk punk language then," I said.

For a moment she was serious. "You're no punk. I've known punks before."

"Oh?"

"I could get to like you, big man. But never a punk." The cab had stopped. I said, "We're here."

"Will I see you again?" Her eyes wanted me to say yes.

"If you say please."

She smiled and touched my mouth with her finger again. "Please."

"I'll call you."

"I'll be waiting. Will you be long?"

"When I find a guy named Lodo."

"Be careful."

"Sure."

She got out and walked away. Her legs were long and her hips wide and with each stride her thighs would play against the fabric of her dress and it was almost as if she had nothing on at all.

I had the cab take me back to DiNuccio's. Art wasn't there, but Joe told me he had called my place a couple times without any luck, then went out.

I grabbed a quick beer, waved to Joe and went out to the corner hoping to catch a crosstown cab.

That was when I knew I had picked up a tail.

He was a small guy in a plastic raincoat with a folded paper sticking up out of the pocket. He hadn't been on the ball and when he first spotted me, his involuntary start tagged him. To make sure, I hesitated on the corner, then turned and walked west. He stayed with me, checking over his shoulder for a cab.

When one came, he caught it, rode to the corner and stopped. I knew he was waiting for me to get the next one and when I passed him he'd hang on. It would've been fun if I had more time. Instead, I turned, went back to the corner and picked up a hack just letting out a passenger. The Brooks Brothers Boys were determined to get their progress report the hard way.

The drizzle turned into a hard rain before I got to the apartment. The street was empty and even Pete-the-Dog was gone to hawk his papers around the bars. I paid off the driver, got my key out and ran for the entrance. I went inside, flipped the light on and knew I had it.

The two sitting there had their rods out smashing slugs over my head and swearing at the dive I had made to one side which put one guy in the way of the other. I rolled once behind a chair, kicked it at them and saw the top rip off it from a slug, then I had my own gun out and cocked and the chubby little guy in front caught a fat .45 dead in the chest. The other one ran for the door and I got him through both knees and he lay there screaming his lungs out until I cracked him across the mouth with the muzzle of the automatic.

He kept saying over and over again. *"Marone, marone!"*

Behind me the other one coughed once, then was still.

I said, "It doesn't really hurt yet. Give it a couple hours."

He pulled his hands away from his knees, looked at the blood and tried to reach for the rod he had dropped. I kicked it out of the way. His eyes were terrible things trying to kill me all by themselves.

I raised the .45 and pointed it at his gut. "Who sent you, bud?"

"Go . . ."

"Watch it. I'm no sweet law-abiding citizen. Knocking you off wouldn't be a bit hard. I even got a license for my rod. Figure it out quick, buddy, because you haven't got much time left at all."

He looked at his hands again and gagged, then fell over on his side. "I need a doctor . . ."

"You'll need an undertaker more."

"Look . . ."

"Talk." My hand started to go white around the butt.

"Ryan . . . it was orders . . . it was . . ." Somehow he knew it was coming. He threw one wild look around before the blast from the doorway caught him. I got out of the line before it could happen to me, then the lights went out and the door slammed shut.

I might have made it at that, but the dead guy in the doorway tripped me and I went down. When I threw the main fuse lever back in place and got outside, there was nobody on the street at all.

The shadows across the street moved a little bit and I went over. Razztazz, the crippled guy, was hunkered back in his basement doorway his shoulders twitching. I said, "You see him, Razz?"

"Went to the corner, Ryan. Soon's you went in a car was standing by. Picked him up."

"You make any of them?"

"One I knew."

"Who?"

"Lardbucket Pearson, the fat guy."

"How'd you know him? You can't see faces from across here now."

"Not by that. It was his big butt and the way he walked. Cop shot him in the behind once. He ain't never walked right since."

"I don't know him, Razz."

"Part of the Jersey crowd where I come from. Always was in the rackets around the docks." He wiped his hand across his face. "They . . . still there?"

"Yeah. Dead."

"Couldn't hear anything from here at all. The fuzz coming along?"

"Let me work it out. Keep it quiet."

"You know me, Ryan."

I stuck a folded bill into his pocket and slapped his shoulder. He grinned and nodded and I went back into the rain.

Neither one of the punks had anything on them at all. No wallets, no labels, no papers of any kind. In their own way they were farsighted pros—but they'd finally walked into the inevitable occupational hazard.

I reloaded the .45, threw a handful of shells in my pocket and looked at them. Things were beginning to look up. It takes a while, but the pattern gets set and starts to look like something. When I had the idea rounded out, I flicked off the light and went out to the vestibule. The rain had made an effective muffler for the sound. There were no curious faces in the windows . . . no movement anywhere, and no sounds of sirens hanging in the air.

At the corner I hung back in the folds of darkness that draped the building there. Traffic was light, nothing more than a few occupied cabs moving with the lights. Nobody was on the sidewalks.

For five minutes I stayed there, watching, then across the street somebody hacked and vomited then painfully unfolded from being a doorway bundle to one of the bums you see around occasionally. He edged toward Second Ave., leaning against the building, then got on his own and wobbled off the curb and started across the street.

Down the block a car pulled away from the curb, flicked on its lights so the beams spotlighted the guy. Just as quickly it cut back to the curb and doused them.

They were waiting for me. Behind me on First would be others.

I was on a kill list now. Someplace along the line I had gotten big enough and important enough to be in somebody's way. Someplace I did something, or I saw something, or I thought something. Someplace I had reached a conclusion that made me ready for the big bed.

Mamie Huggins never bothered to lock her basement entrance. I took a chance on not being seen and went back and down through her basement. There was one low fence to cross and I came out the alley between Benny's grocery and the building they were tearing down.

When the block was empty, I crossed again and used the alley where Jamie Tohey kept his laundry pushcarts. I went all the way through, turned west when I reached the street and went back to Second again. Up near my own corner the car still waited. I grinned at it and walked south to Hymie's drug store.

After five tries I reached Art through his office and told him what had happened. Tension was evident in his voice when he asked me what I wanted.

I said, "Get me what you can on a character named Lardbucket Pearson. He'll probably have Jersey connections."

"Sure. What about the stiffs in your apartment? You can't let 'em lie there and it's damn sure nobody's going to just stumble over them."

"Why don't you do it, Art?"

"Do what?"

"Make a call at my place and find them. Any one of the sheets would buy a news beat with photos for the bit."

"You crazy? Listen . . ."

"You listen. Do it. Otherwise I'll call a guy with the wire services. Give me twenty-four hours to think, then do it."

He breathed hard into the receiver before he answered me. "Okay, friend, but it's blood money. You'll have the cops screaming for your hair."

"That'll make it unanimous."

"Where can I get in touch with you?"

"Use the Naples Cafe on Second Street. They'll take any messages."

I hung up, reached for the phone book and flipped through it until I found the only Carmen Smith and dialed the number. I let it ring a good while before I hung up feeling a little sour.

The other number was Jake McGaffney. He wasn't doing anything and said to come on up. It took me 20 minutes and my feet got soaking wet.

He looked at my face and said, "Wha' hoppen, boy?"

I told him. He made himself a drink and opened me a beer.

"This hitting my business, Ryan?"

"I don't think so. If that tap on Gonzales didn't do it, then you're clear enough."

"You're trying to make a point someplace."

"Where was Gonzales collecting for you?"

"Oh, light spots, mostly. He had a string of bars . . . let's say about twenty, and a few other places in his own neighborhood."

"Did he work around the docks?"

"Gonzales? Hell, no. I'm not doing any field work in that area. That's uptown stuff."

"That's what I thought. How much did he usually have on hand?"

Jake shrugged and made a face. "He'd pay off two-three hundred every day, bring back five. Small time, but with plenty small guys working, we stay in business y'know?"

"Was he square?"

"A dream to have working. Never clipped a dime, and that I know." He sipped at his drink. "What's all this traffic with Gonzales, Ryan?"

"He had a dream too . . . of him and his broad taking a trip around the world, really living it up."

"*Him?* On what? He never had anything."

"He had ten grand."

"Hell, you can't even do Miami right on ten . . ." He stopped, put his drink down and stared at me. "Where'd he get ten grand?"

"I think from a guy named Billings."

"I don't get it."

"Don't worry about it. Neither do I. One other thing. Does the name Lodo mean anything to you?"

Jake's memory for names was too good for him to think long. He shook his head and there was nothing more to say.

The cabs were slower now. I saw one stopped for the light, ran across the street and climbed in. The address I gave was Lucinda Gonzales' and when I got out the street was quiet, like a sick dog.

There was a light on under Lucinda's door and when I knocked a chair scraped back.

She smiled vacantly and I could smell the whiskey on her. I pushed the door shut behind me and said, "Lucinda?"

"You still have your money?"

She sat down heavily and brushed her hair back. "Si . . . but it is no good now without Juan."

"Lucinda . . . who has been here to see you?"

"To see me? Oh . . . the neighbors. They come. From uptown my cousin, he comes."

"Any of Juan's friends?"

"They are peegs, señor."

"Do you know who they are?"

"Sure." She swayed and tried to get up. "They are off the boat." She leaned hard against the table, balancing herself. "One is 'Fredo. Other is Spanish Tom. They are peegs, señor. They theenk I am listening to them and they hit me. Juan, he does not even care."

I circled the table and held on to her. "What boat, Lucinda?"

She shrugged and reached for the bottle. Her unsteady hand knocked it over and she started to cry. I eased her back into the chair and let her pass out with her head pressed into her forearms.

When I reached Times Square, I stopped, deciding which hotel to use. I settled on the Chessy on 49th and took off that way. Before I reached the end of the first block, I knew I had somebody behind me.

He came up fast, passed me and said, "Ryan," without turning his head. He crossed against the lights, hesitated, then jay-walked all the way to the east side of the street.

When nobody could have made any connection I crossed over myself, went down to 47th and turned the corner leisurely. Then I stopped and flattened against the wall.

Nothing. I gave it another two minutes before I went to where Diego Flores was waiting for me in the shadows.

He was more scared than nervous and his beady little eyes kept poking into the night on either side of him. Diego ran numbers for Sid Solomon on the Madison Avenue run and usually he was a pretty calm guy.

I said, "Hi, Dago. What's the fuss?"

He tapped my chest with a forefinger. "Baby . . . you got rocks in your head. Big fat rocks. What you doin' in town?"

"Why leave, kid?"

"Ain't you heard it yet? Ryan baby, what happened to all those big ears you had?"

"I'm listening now."

"Baby . . . whoever throws you down makes five grand. The word's out on you."

"Who says, Dago?"

"None of our bunch, baby. This one's comin' in the hard way. It's all over town. First thing, the nose candy kids'll be tryin' for the tap. You got marked poison somehow and unless you blow out you're dead."

"Where's it come from?"

"Picked it up at Bimmy's. You know Stan Etching?" I nodded and he went on. "Him and that nutty brother of his was talkin' about it. Since they knocked off Fletcher over in Canarsie they're big stuff. Anyway, they're working now and you're their job. Everybody's gonna be trying for you, baby."

"Why not you, Dago?"

"Ah, baby, come off it. You favored me up plenty times when I had troubles."

"How hot is it?"

"You better not go anyplace you're known. They even got the hotels spotted. You're a big one."

"Okay, kid, thanks. Shove off before you get tied in to me."

He glanced around again and licked his lips. "Baby . . . be careful, will ya? I can smell this stink. It's from way up, ya know? Ya can tell, somethin's burning in this town."

"Yeah."

When he walked off, I gave him five minutes and cruised past the Chessy. I spotted Manny Golden in the foyer and his partner Willis Holmes across the street talking to a cab driver outside the Ployden House. Both were ex-cops busted out in the graft scandal in '49. Now they were hoods. Not cheap ones, either. They still held a few things over important precinct heads and could move around pretty good when they wanted to.

Just to be sure I made a few of the other pads off Broadway and when I saw Mario Sen, I knew just how hot I was. Mario's specialty was big kills and he didn't operate for under 10 grand per. That is, outside his regular job.

Mario was a tap man for the Mafia.

Mario didn't seem to have any place to go specially so I helped him out. I stuck my gun in his back and steered him in to the men's room in the back of the lobby.

He was real embarrassed.

I let him turn around and have a good look at me and said, "You got yourself a big one this time, buddy." Then I smashed him across the face with the rod and when he went down choking noisily, I whipped the gun across his skull until he stopped.

He was going to be a sick hood. Sicker when his boss found out.

The envelope held an even grand in fifties. It fitted my pocket nicely. There was nothing new about the rest of the contents. They were photos of me. Police photos. Something Golden or Holmes dug up, probably. I flushed them down the toilet, frisked Mario and lifted another $400 from his poke and added it to my pile.

It was turning out to be a good evening.

I grabbed a cab outside, went to 23rd St., walked crosstown two blocks and took another one back. The third one let me out on the corner of Carmen Smith's block.

I told the officious little man at the desk I wished to see Miss Smith and that it was important enough that he should call and waken her. He didn't believe me at first, then I smiled and he believed me.

Carmen answered the house phone, asked to speak to me and when I said hello, told me to come right up. The little man was still nervous so I put her on and let her tell him it was okay. He clacked his teeth and escorted me to the elevator and showed me which button to push. I said thanks and pushed it.

She was waiting in the tiny foyer that separated her apartment from the elevator. She said, "Well, hello! And if you don't mind the obvious, what brings you here?"

I grinned at her. "I need a place to sleep."

"Oh," she said, and opened the door wide. "Come on in."

She had on a tailored, double-breasted housecoat that fitted without a fold or a crease and when she walked, the static of her body against the cloth made it cling so that you knew she slept cool and naked and inviting.

Like beautiful girls should be, she was unruffled from sleep, still bearing the flush of lipstick. She walked ahead of me into the living room and she was tall even without shoes. When she turned on the light on the end table, there was a momentary silhouette that made me stop and look around quickly, merely sensing the expensive appointments of the place rather than appreciating them.

Carmen looked at me quizzically a moment. Then she *knew*. She smiled gently and waved me to a chair. She brought a drink without a word, handed it to me and sat down.

Then, very deliberately, she grinned and crossed her legs.

I could have smacked her in the mouth.

She said, "Okay, hood, what do you want from me?" Then her grin turned into a small laugh that made the mood easier.

"Kid, you can get in real trouble doing that."

"You mean the leg action."

"Don't get smart."

She made a kiss with her mouth and blew it across the room. "Now really, why did you come up?"

"I'm in a bind."

The smile softened, then worked into a frown. "Police?"

"A little worse, sugar. The sign's on me."

She didn't need any explanation. She took a few seconds letting it sink in and there was something tight about the way she held herself. "Bad?"

"Real bad. They called out the troops."

Her eyes crinkled thoughtfully. She got up, took my glass and refilled it. When she handed it to me, she said, "Will it help to tell me?"

"No, but I will." And I told her.

She sat wordlessly a moment, then: "What can I do, Ryan?"

"Pack me in for the night, kitten, I don't like to be shot when I'm sleeping, and all my usual pads are off limits now."

"That's all?" She stood up and studied me with the edge of her forefinger between her teeth.

I stood up too and took her hand away. "No, there's more, but I wouldn't inflict it on you, sugar."

She was there in my arms without seeming to move. Suddenly she was just there, pressing tightly against me and she was warm and woman and I could feel the life inside her. Her finger touched my mouth, then her own. "Why, Ryan?"

Softly, I said, "For a hood I got certain sensitivities."

She reached up and kissed me lightly. She smiled, did it again and took my arm under hers. She showed me the guest room and opened the door.

Once more she came back into my arms. "I have certain sensitivities too. I wish you would inflict them on me."

"Later."

Her mouth was warm and very wet. "All right, later." Lightly, she touched my lips with her tongue, deliberately tantalizing.

Her grin got impish and she did something with her hands. Then she shrugged and handed me the housecoat, stepped back and smiled again. She walked away from me into the light, turned into her room and was gone.

When I began to breathe again, I tossed the housecoat on a chair, took a real cold shower and went to bed. Before I could sleep my mind dwelt on the litheness of her, the swaying stride, the lush, yet muscular curves that seemed to melt into each other and dance in the subdued, shadowy tones of dark and light. Brunette, I thought, a luscious, chestnut-hued brunette.

The radio alarm beside the bed went off softly. Awakening, I knew where I was at once, knowing, too, that I had never set the alarm. But the door was partly open and the housecoat gone, so I knew who had. The note on the clock was brief. It said, *Call me, hood.* And the P.S. was just as brief. She had written, *You look pretty.*

There were no covers on the bed and now we were even for the housecoat.

Coffee was ready in the electric perc and there were some Danish in a basket. While I grabbed a bite, I called the Naples Cafe, got a number for me to call Art and dialed it.

In the background there were morning noises of people eating, and strange, loud languages. There was juke music and somebody yelling and Art was drunk. He was all-night drunk, but purpose-drunk and there's a difference. He felt his way through his words, mouthing each one. "Ryan . . . I got what you wanted."

"Good. Let's have it."

"You see the papers?"

"Not yet."

"Those punks . . . you hit . . . your place?"

"Yeah?"

"Cullen and . . . and Stanovich. From Elizabeth, Jersey, y'know? Muscle boys . . . docks. This here . . . Lardbucket Pearson . . . him . . . I mean, he and Turner Scado's car piled into . . . big ditch outside Hoboken. They got killed. Looks like your boys . . . muff it, they get it."

The picture was clear enough. It even made the deal bigger than ever. When somebody can afford to knock off help who flubbed, it was big time, real big-time.

I said, "What's their connections, Art?"

He fumbled against the phone for a second. "Topside. Big. It reaches, Ryan. Goes far . . . to . . . to Europe."

"What names, kid?"

I could hear ice clink in a glass, then he paused to swallow. He finally said, "Those Jersey Joes . . . Mafia musclemen. Used to be part of . . . Lucky's crew. You know what that means?"

"It's making sense. What else?"

He laughed sourly. "I'm gonna . . . beat you . . . on this one, Irish. I have a friend in Rome. Good friend. In their organization over there. For . . . American cash . . . he's tipping me to your mysterious buddy."

"What buddy?"

"Lodo," he chuckled. "Lodo . . . pretty big stuff. Lodo's . . . code name for Mafia's East Coast enforcer. Big killer. Little while I'll know who."

I said, "Okay. Go home and stay there. You hear?"

"I'll go slow." He paused a moment, coughed and said, "You're lucky, Irish."

"How?"

"You're going to get to die real . . . soon."

I hopped a cab to 34th St., picked up an envelope at General Delivery in the Post Office and opened it on the street.

The laddies were real efficient. Usually it took a month to get a gun permit. This one came through quick. I tucked it in my pocket and looked at the other slip of paper. There were seven digits there, and the first two had to be exchange letters. I found a pay phone and dialed.

A male voice said, "Yes?"

I said, "Big Man?"

He said, "That you, Ryan?"

"Me. And don't trace this."

His voice sounded strained. "What do you need, Irish?"

"Two guys. They work a ship that was in around the week a certain Juan Gonzales was killed. All I know is the alias. One's Spanish Tom, the other 'Fredo . . . probably Alfredo. You big enough to handle it?"

"We're big enough."

I left the booth, walked to the corner and had two minutes before the unmarked cruiser drew up and the guys hopped out. Another one blocked off the street at the other end and a fast, systematic search started. I laughed at the slobs and walked away. Big Man was playing both ends from the middle.

I gave him an hour. It was plenty of time. They had men and equipment and millions and could do nearly any damn thing they wanted when they wanted.

I called and said, "Big Man?"

He said, "Both men are on the *Gastry*. It's in port now. Spanish Tom is Tomas Escalante. The other one is Alfredo Lias. Both from Lisbon. They've been on the same ship since '46. Both have had numerous drunk arrests in various ports but nothing more serious. The line vouches for their honesty."

"Thanks. You haven't bothered to look for them, have you?"

He caught the sarcasm. "They're in port, Ryan. We've been looking but so far we haven't found them."

I laughed. "What would you ask them if you did?"

"We'd think of something."

"Good for you," I said. "There's just one more thing

I never bothered asking. You guys don't operate without certain facts or at the most without ideas."

"So?"

"What did you suspect Billings of having for sale?"

Quietly, he said, "A month ago two skin divers were killed going down on the wreck of the *Andrea Doria*."

"I read about it."

"There were three on the expedition. The last one hasn't shown."

"Go on."

"It should be obvious. Highly classified material went down in that wreck and if found by the wrong parties could jeopardize the safety of the whole country. Possibly the whole world."

After a moment he said, "That enough?"

I said, "That's enough," and hung up.

Nobody was outside and I walked away from the phone thinking about it. There were just too many possibilities now. Some of them had to go. I walked slowly and let things dribble through my mind. A pattern began to come out of it.

Further down the street I stepped into another phone booth, rang the apartment to see if Art was there. I let it ring a dozen times then decided he was either asleep or passed out, then gave up.

I picked up a paper from a newstand. They had given me pretty good coverage. Pictures and all.

Police opinion seemed to be that it was a gang killing of some kind, that I had been poaching in foreign fields. There was speculation that I had been taken for an old-fashioned ride. So far their leads were lousy.

So was their liaison. The big agency upstairs that had conned me into this rumble wasn't talking either.

Natural coloration is the animal's best protection. In the slop chutes that were the playgrounds for the dock crowd I fitted smooth and easy. They could smell money on you, they knew you were brand new to the neighborhood, but all the time they knew the other thing they saw in your face. You just weren't takeable.

A couple I knew, tough apples who'd work any kind of a touch for pocket money. They passed me over with a nod and gave me room at the bar.

If the word was out all the way, it hadn't reached here yet. But maybe they were figuring it the usual way . . . a hood hates to leave his own back yard. Every

step away from his own hole and he becomes more
vulnerable. His own distorted sense of security that led
him into a hole in the first place makes him stay close
to it even when he's dying.

There could be another reason too. New York was a
big town. The word can only travel just so fast . . . and
it wasn't good to think about it. Any time now the posters
could go up and in this section hired guns were handy
to get to.

The pair I spoke to on the *Gastry* didn't have much
to say about Escalante or Lias. As far as they knew, all
they did in port was visit around the Spanish-speaking
sections and get gassed up. Neither had steady women
or much to do with the rest of the crew.

Neither one of them was very smart. Both were dull,
plodding types who were at the peak of their earning
capacity in the grimy hold of the freighter.

It just didn't figure right. They weren't 10-grand types.
They weren't international types. They weren't the type
anybody should get excited about or interested in for
any damn reason whatsoever. Their being around at all
had all the earmarks of a crazy, distracting coincidence
like a fly in the soup but until I found them I couldn't
be sure.

A long time ago I learned how to get answers without
ever having to ask the questions. But it took time. It
took me from 57th Street down to the Battery and halfway back and by then it was night again with the same
damn rain thick with dirt and soot that steamed up from
the pavement and got inside your clothes.

But I found Spanish Tom. He was in the middle of a
crowd of dock workers and the center of attraction, sitting on the pavement with his back against the overhead
highway support and if you didn't see the hole in him
right away you'd think he was sleeping.

The uniformed cop taking notes squatted and held his
coat open with the tip of his pencil and for a moment
everybody quieted down and craned to see the business
better. It was quite a tap, a real professional job, one hard
knife jab under the ribs and up into the heart and that
was the end.

I worked my way through to the front and stood there
trying to figure the angle on it. I kind of started a trend
and a few more wanted in close and when the cop
stood up he yelled for everybody to get the hell away. He

scared the half-drunk sailor beside me and he nudged the body and Spanish Tom flopped sideways on the pavement and one leg kicked out like he was still alive.

The cop yelled again and shoved the nearest ones away. He turned to me, but by then I had already backed off and the pasteboard ticket that had come out of Spanish Tom's pocket was under my foot. I scraped it back, retrieved it, and squeezed back through the crowd.

In the one second I saw it I had thought it was a pawn slip, but when I got back under the light I could have spit. It was an ADMIT TWO in Spanish to some shindig up in the quarter. I crumbled it in my fist and threw it back in the gutter and mouthed a curse at it.

Then I thought about it again and picked it up. If Alfredo Lias had one of these too it could be the place he'd be at. The date was tomorrow; the place a bloody-up with an olê olê band. The clientele was the kind you saw in the tabloids leaning up against a wall while the fuzz frisked them.

But that was tomorrow. I had *now* to think about. Until tomorrow I had to stay out of sight of everybody and it wasn't going to be easy. I flagged a cab down, gave an address a block away from Art's and got out on an empty corner.

Halfway down I found the Wheeler Apartments and touched Art's bell. The vestibule door was open so before he could answer I went ahead up. I knocked at his door and waited, knocked again and listened for him stirring around.

There wasn't a sound from inside.

I tried the door and the knob turned under my hand. I pushed it open, stepped inside, shut it behind me and waited there in the semi-gloom of the room. It was too still, much too still. I pulled the .45 out already cocked and held it ready, then flicked on the light.

Nothing.

It wasn't much of a place. Something a bachelor would have. One main room with the kitchen separated from it by a bar, an open door leading to the bath and another door, cracked a little, going to the bedroom.

I walked over to that one, pushed it open the rest of the way and reached for the light switch inside the frame.

And then I found Art.

The spare pillow beside him showed powder burns and one corner had been ripped off from the bullet blast the pillow had muffled. It had caught him in the temple and without ever realizing it Art had reached the goal he had striven for.

All I could say was one word. There was nothing else. I was being hung higher all the time. Nobody knew I told Art to make a feature yarn out of the kills at my place and now the fuzz would lay this tap at my door and label it a revenge kill. Whoever coined the word *shafted* had me in mind.

There was a whiskey, cordite and burnt feathers smell still in the air, a smell that could hang for hours. I felt Art's face, knew by the heat of it that death came only a short time ago. I went back to the door to see if it had been forced, but there were no marks around the lock. Art had made it easy for the killer. He had come home drunk, opened up and shut the door. The lock was a type you had to hand turn from the inside to latch and he had done what a thousand other drunks did before him. He forgot about it. He flopped in bed and that was it.

I went through his pockets carefully, tried his jacket thrown over a chair, then the clothes in the closet. There was something not quite orderly enough about the clothes in his dresser and I knew that all this had been done earlier by an expert and if there had been anything important, it was gone now.

I wiped the spots I had touched with my handkerchief and backed out of the apartment. I went upstairs and over the roof to a building near the corner and came out there in case anybody was waiting for me outside Art's place. Two blocks further down I found a cab and gave him Carmen's number.

The important little man remembered me from before, but even then he double-checked. He told me reluctantly that Miss Smith would see me, then huffed away, so supreme in his own importance that he never recognized me even with the paper on his desk open to my picture.

I went upstairs to where she was waiting and grinned at the worry that showed around her eyes. Then suddenly she was tight inside my arms and her mouth was a hungry thing tasting me almost painfully, her body taut with life that has been confined too long and for the first time senses a release.

Tears made glistening streaks down her cheeks and

when she took her mouth from mine she kept it open, sobbing against my neck.

I said, "Easy, baby," and held her away to look at her, but only for a second because she grabbed me again and hung on fiercely.

Very softly she repeated over and over, "You crazy hood. You crazy hood, you!"

I wiped off the tears, kissed her lightly, then took her arm and went inside. There was still a sob in her breathing and she wasn't ready to talk to me yet. I said, "I'm not used to such pleasant receptions."

She forced a smile, then it became real. "You crazy Irishman. Every paper, every TV newscaster, every radio broadcast has you in it. Ryan . . . you haven't got a chance . . . you haven't . . . I don't know how to put it . . ."

"It's bad, huh?"

"Why, Ryan? Why does it have to be you?"

"Why all the concern, sugar?"

She said nothing for a moment. Her eyes frowned and she took her hand from mine and folded them in her lap. "I'm not the type who should do something like this. I know better. I've been familiar with . . . wrong situations a whole lifetime. It's never happened before. Now, for the first time I know what it's like, having to . . . care for somebody who feels nothing, well, very special about you. It's happened to others. I never thought it could possibly happen to me." She looked up, smiled and added lightly, "And with a hood too. I've never been in love with a hood before."

"You're crazy."

"I know," she said.

"You're class, baby. With me a fling could be fun. Some excitement, like playing cards, maybe. But sugar . . . like I'm not the kind of slob kids like you fall in love with. You're class."

"Irish . . . you've never had trouble getting a woman . . . ever. Have you?"

I squinted and shook my head. "Tomatoes, though."

"So let me be a tomato. Or should I ask please?"

"You're talking crazy, girl."

"I have nothing else, Irish. I never had."

"Hell, I could be cut down any time. You know what that means? You get connected with me and you're done, kid. Done. Maybe it's like you said . . . you've never been in love with a hood before, but it's like the excitement of drawing three cards from the dealer and finding yourself with a royal flush. It's great if the stakes are high, but when the other hands are twos and threes and go out on a small pot the big excitement is all wasted. It only seemed big. It wasn't worth anything. Damn it, you're crazy!"

I was tight on talk and that scar on my back began to draw up again. I had to tell her. She knew what the score was!

Carmen's eyes were clear now. While I was talking she had made up her mind. She said, "Will you let me be a crazy tomato, Irish?"

"Kitten . . ."

"You don't have to love me back at all," she said.

I tried hard to keep it inside. I didn't want to let it out, but it wasn't the kind of thing you can squash into pieces and forget. "That's the bad part, kid," I told her. "You see . . . I do."

She was there in my arms again, softly at first and hungry-mouthed again. Her fingers were velvet cat claws, kneading me gently, searching and finding. When I touched her, things seemed to melt away until there was only the warmth of flesh and a giddy sensation of being overpowered by a runaway emotion. As I lay there, time ceased to exist and as she came down on top of me she murmured little things only the mind heard and it was different. So very different.

Morning was a soft light that bathed us both, and we got up smiling, yet saying nothing. Words were no good any more. I watched her shower and dress. All the naked, all the clothed beauty of her belonged to me and nobody could take it away.

Then the luxury of sleep-drugged morning was over and I knew how stupid it was and the vomit sour taste of cold hate for all the things that had happened to me was in my mouth.

I dressed quickly and followed her into the kitchen. She had coffee ready and handed me a cup, knowing by my face that something was wrong. She didn't ask. She waited until I was ready. I said, "I had a friend who was killed last night. I know how, I know why and I know who, but I don't know what the killer's face is like."

"Can I help somehow?"

"You can but I won't ask you. The gamble is too big."

"You forgot, Irish?"

"What?"

"I *am* a gambler."

"That kill is going to be laid at my feet and there isn't a chance in the world for me to cut out."

"The police . . ."

"Can be stalled a while. They can be stymied, but only for a while. When they concentrate all the resources of their system, they can do anything."

"You think they will?"

"They have to, baby. Now it's a newshawk who's dead and the papers will hammer the brass silly. They have to shake that heat and the only way is to find me."

"But first we gamble."

I looked at her hard. She wasn't kidding. I said, "Okay, baby, it'll be you and me. We'll give it a try. Maybe we can make the good parts come out."

"What will we do?"

"Tonight's Saturday night, kid. We're going dancing." A puzzled frown creased her forehead. "You'll need a costume for the act, sugar. Where we'll be you'll want the West Side trollop look. Think you can make it?"

She nodded, the frown deepening.

"A missing link was killed last night," I continued. "He had a dance ticket in his pocket. Chances are his partner had one too. On top of which, if he knows his buddy's dead, he'll want to be with a crowd. It's easy to die alone."

"This one . . . he can clear you?"

I grinned at that one. "Not him. But this bird can supply a lot of answers."

"Then what can I do?"

"First you can go out and buy some clothes. Cheap and flashy. Get perfume and accessories to match and if you can get the stuff secondhand, do that. Guys alone at those jumps can't move around the way a couple can and locating this guy will be easier with two of us asking questions."

I took her shoulders and looked into her eyes. "Still want to try it?"

She grinned impishly, made like she was going to give me a tiny kiss, then stuck her tongue in my mouth. Before my hands could tighten on her she pulled away and went to the door.

"You'll stay here?"

"I don't know."

She opened her purse, took out a key and tossed it

to me. "If you come in the back way you can by-pass the clerk." She blew a kiss and was gone.

I got up, yanked my coat on and shoved the .45 under my belt. I went out the back way and headed for the old brownstone. The sun died before I reached Sixth and the air had a cold, clammy touch to it. I stopped at a candy store and had a Coke, then another, trying to think the pieces together.

A pattern was there, all right. Crude and irregular, but it had a purpose.

Outside it began to rain again.

A beat cop sauntered by and looked in, but I was in the shadows and my face didn't mean a thing to him. When he was gone, I picked up my change and walked out, my collar up around my neck, the hatbrim screening my face.

I was almost at Lexington when they had me. It worked real easy, the faint nudge of a gun barrel in a hand with a paper around it and that was all there was to it.

I looked around and Stan Etching was smiling at me, the scar on his chin pulling his mouth out of shape. He said, "They told me you were a tough guy, Ryan." He stepped around in front of me, lifted out the gun and dropped it in his raincoat pocket.

His smile was nervous and I knew what he was thinking. It was almost too easy. I said, "Now what?"

"You'll see. My brother Stash saw me grab you, feller. He'll be here with the car in a minute. Maybe you'd like it better to run or something."

I grinned and his eyes got nervous along with his mouth. "I'll wait," I said.

The car was a three-year-old Caddie sedan with Jersey plates. It pulled up noiselessly and Stan opened the back door. I got in and he sat on my right, his gun pointed at my belly.

When we pulled away from the curb Stash turned the radio up and said, "How'd he take it?"

"Like pie. How else?" He poked me with the gun and grinned. "You're a chump, Ryan. You shoulda hid out. Me, I knew you'd come back though. Six of us had your dump staked out, but I even knew which way you'd come."

"This is the old Chicago touch you're giving it," I said. "One way ride and all that crap."

He laughed. "Sure. Glad you don't feel bad about it.

Hey Stash, this guy's all right." The gun bumped me again. "You know, Ryan, I'm gonna burn you out quick. No fooling around. You give me no trouble, I give you no trouble."

I told him thanks and leaned back in the seat and watched Stash approach the Lincoln Tunnel. Traffic was heavy.

Stan looked across at me and grinned again, turning a little to point the rod square at me. I took a deep breath of disgust, leaned back further into the cushions and completely relaxed.

Then I moved my hand before he could pull the trigger, slammed back the slide on the automatic so it couldn't fire, twisted it so his finger broke and while he was still screaming with surprise and pain, shoved the muzzle against his gut and pulled the trigger.

Up front Stash let out a crazy startled yell and tried to look back, but there wasn't a thing he could do, not a damn, stinking thing. I got my .45 back from Stan, cocked it and let Stash feel the big "O" of the mouth of it against his neck. His head jerked like a spastic's and he kept making funny little noises.

I said, "When we get out, I'll tell you where to go. Don't do anything silly."

He didn't. He stayed calmly hysterical and when we reached the scrap iron works in Secaucus, we stopped and I let him get in the back. The shock was wearing off and Stan's face was white with pain and fear. He kept asking for a doctor, but I shook my head.

Stash said, "What'cha gonna do?"

"It depends on you. I want to know about the word. Who put it out?"

Stash looked hopelessly at his brother. Stan said, ". . . doctor."

"Not yet. Maybe when you talk a little."

It began to dawn on Stan gradually. I wasn't kidding. He shook his head feebly. "I told ya. Nothin'. You know . . . how them things are."

I raised the gun again and watched his eyes. He couldn't even speak, but he was telling it straight. I said, "Who else is around my place and where?"

"Golden . . . and Holmes. They're on the south end. Lou Steckler, he's . . . across in . . . in the gimp's house."

My hand got tight on the gun. "What'd they do to Razztazz?"

"Jeez . . . I dunno . . . I . . ."

"Who else? Dammit, talk fast!"

"Mario . . . he's in your dump."

"No fuzz?"

"Nobody. They . . . they got pulled off. Hymie the Goose, he's covering trains and all with his bunch. Babcock and . . . the Greek . . . they . . . Jersey. They . . ."

He fainted then. I gave him five minutes and let him come around. He started to retch and vomited all down his chest. Stash was still hysterical and shook all over.

I said, "What else, Stan?"

He shook his head.

There wasn't any more and I knew it. I told Stash to get out of the car and walk around the side. I had him pull his brother out and they stood there like animals watching me. I said, "Whenever and wherever I see you again, you catch one between the antlers, buddies. I don't think I'll have to worry about it because somebody else will get to you first like with them Elizabeth hoods. Now beat it."

Stan's eyes went wide. "Jeez . . . ain't you even gonna call a doc? Ain't you . . ."

"They were right when they said I was a tough guy."

"Ryan . . . Ryan . . ."

I started the car up. "Drop dead," I told him.

I took the car back through the tunnel and parked it on a cross street. When I wiped the wheel, door handles and sills off I climbed out and left it there. I found a phone, dialed the number I wanted and said, "Big Man?"

"Ryan . . ."

"Okay, Big Man, just listen for once. Where can we meet?"

"It's no good."

"Brother, I'm going to blow the whistle if you don't square off."

He paused. He didn't muffle the phone to talk to anyone or anything. He just sat there a minute, then: "We'll see you."

"Just you, friend."

"Where?"

"The Naples Cafe. It's on . . ."

"I know."

"Okay, then. Have a squad standing by a phone, but first you come alone. Quick."

He hung up without answering. I hopped a cab to the Naples and stood across the street. In 10 minutes another cab came along and the big man got out. He walked inside and when I was fairly certain nobody else was around, I crossed over and went inside. He was sitting there at a table with a cup of coffee in front of him, waiting.

I said, "It's not so snotty like the first time, is it?"

His face was hard. "Let's hear it, Ryan."

For some reason I wasn't edgy any more. I put my face in my hands and rubbed hard, then leaned on the table and stared at him. "Art Shay was killed," I said.

He nodded again. "We know. The police think you did it."

"Who found him?"

"Young kid upstairs who used his typewriter. Trying to be a free-lance writer. He's clean."

"So am I. No alibi. No proof. I'm just saying."

He tried one on me for size. "Spanish Tom showed up."

"Yeah, dead."

"You get around. We squelched the story."

"I was there right after it happened."

His eyes slitted a little bit. "What did you know about him?"

"Nothing, but I'll damn soon find out."

"How?"

"I'm pretty sure I know where his partner will be to-night."

"You want to tell me?"

"Not me, Big Man. I'm going all the way on this party."

"All right, Ryan, what did you want to call this . . . this meeting for?"

I sat back and sucked in my breath. "I want some answers. I want them straight and to the point. I have a funny feeling that I've touched something someplace and I'm close to what I want. I never did like any part of this business, but I'm in it all the way and if I want to stay alive and you want to get your answers, check me off with the truth."

He made a short gesture with his hand. "Go ahead."

"Was I suckered into this thing with big talk or because I was suspect?"

For a moment he looked at my face, then made his decision. "A little of both. You were suspect because you were brought into it by Billings. We had to grasp at straws no matter how small."

"Why?"

"You know why. Whatever Billings had was an international affair. The underworld of two continents was breaking out the war drums. We knew something was developing but we didn't know why, where or how."

"And how far are you now?"

The smile he gave me was cold. "In our own way we have made progress." I waited and smiled back, just as cold. If he wanted anything, then he couldn't afford to stop. He knew it and said, "Coincidence is the killer of men."

"It's late for philosophy."

"Yes, it is. We know something about Spanish Tom and Lias. We can guess at what happened."

I swung at a wild one. "They overheard something they shouldn't've."

The swing connected and big man squinted at me. He nodded, then went on. "A dock watchman remembered them drinking behind some bales of rags. It wasn't too uncommon and it was easier letting them sleep it off than fight them off so he just forgot it.

"Later he was pulled away by someone yelling for help in the water and it took about an hour to drag some dame out who apparently didn't want to go. She stalled as long as she could. Our guess is that it was a feint to get the watchman off so a plant could be made on the *Gastry*.

"We figure that sometime during the action, either Escalante or Lias overheard or saw what was going on and figured it for the usual smuggling bit and thought they could step into the play and make a fast buck for themselves."

"How could you confirm it?" I asked.

"At that time Spanish customs, acting with *Interpol*, cracked down hard on all points. Nothing was getting out by the usual routes and four big outfits were broken up. Still, traffic had to get through and it's well known that these operations all have emergency plans and in this case one went into effect. Whatever it was couldn't stay in Lisbon without being uncovered sooner or later so the *Gastry* became the transporter."

"Who was involved on board?"

"Nobody. These affairs are not of the moment. They're set up far in advance. Undoubtedly the *Gastry* was fitted with a hiding place a long time ago to be used when necessary and without anyone on board being the wiser.

When in the other port another operative would remove the shipment by preconceived plan. These groups are pretty smart. They're big business. Even big government. We checked out every man on the *Gastry* so far and they're clean. Lias and Escalante were there by coincidence. Some time we'll strip the ship down and find out how it was done."

"That brings us to Billings."

The big man looked across the table at me, the question in his eyes a genuine one. "Do you know how, Irish?"

"I think so."

"Are you going to wait to tell me?"

"No." I let all the pieces come together slowly and began to fit them in place. I said, "Through a language association the two met a guy named Juan Gonzales. They mentioned what they had and wanted a buyer. Juan got greedy all of a sudden, I think. He knew he could buy for peanuts and sell big. Maybe the two knew what a good going price was and kept it fairly high. Anyway, Juan knew the guy with the loot who was looking for a touch. Bil' gs had ten grand of ready money. He let Juan make the buy, probably on a partnership basis. Later he killed him and had the buy for himself. Juan was a scared lad. Maybe he knew he was set up to be tapped off. Billings was scared too. The original owners wanted possession and were going after it. Billings couldn't run fast enough. They caught him. He went out letting me hold the bag."

"Who was it, Irish? Who is Lodo?"

"Art died because he was about to find out. Lodo was the code name for the Mafia enforcer on the East Coast here."

He didn't say anything. It didn't seem to register on him.

"It's important, isn't it?" I said.

"Maybe. The Mafia is a catchall term sometimes. It's still big, but sometimes is the patsy for other big outfits. We have leads into most of the Mafia sections and haven't heard of this angle yet."

"There's always something new," I told him. "Now . . . how new was what I told you?"

"New enough. It's going to change our operation." He paused, stared at me and rubbed his chin with his fist. "You left out some parts, Irish."

"Like what?"

"Why everybody wants you dead."

I let him see my teeth. "I wish I knew. When I do, I'll have your Lodo, laddie."

"Maybe you've done enough right now."

He saw more teeth. "No no, daddy-o. Remember in the beginning . . . that big bundle of bills? I want them. I got plans."

"Care to talk about them?"

"No. But I will give you something to look at. Whoever wants me has my place staked out. Some of those boys you'd like to have and you can get them if you try putting a decoy into my pad. It could prove real interesting."

"We know where they are. We even had it in mind. We were there when the Etchings picked you up this morning."

"My mouth must have hung open. "Damn," I said. "That was a ride. Why didn't you move in?"

He shrugged casually. "I didn't call it because I knew you'd come out of the trap. By the way, where are they now?"

I played it just as casually. "Someplace in Jersey and Stan Etching has a hole in his gut."

"Fine," he said. "I'll put it down as a verbal report."

He stood up and said, "Be careful tonight. If you need help, you can call."

"Sure," I said. "Sure."

It was 3:35 and the day hadn't changed yet. I waited in the doorway until a cab showed with his toplight on and I flagged him down. I rode up to where the *Peter F. Hanes III, Co., Inc.* was out of sight 16 floors up and gave the business to the elevator boy. He looked at me, shrugged and sent the car up.

The place was quiet. From some distant room came the soft clack of a typewriter and from another angle there was the muted monotone of someone on the telephone. An unmarked door beside the reception desk opened and the redhead came out, saw me and grinned all over. She was in tight green and knew what it was doing for her. "I could hope you came to see me but I know you didn't."

"How come you work on Saturdays?"

"Only some Saturdays. It's quiet then and on busy seasons you can catch up."

"I get the kick. Carmen here?"

"Miss Smith?"

I shook my head. "Carmen. We're buddies."

Her eyes flicked away, then came back annoyed a moment before the smile touched them again. "Second best. That's how I always come out. No, she's not here. She was shopping and was in and out a couple of times. Did you call her home?"

"Uh-uh."

She reached for the phone and dialed a number. I heard it ring about a half a dozen times then the redhead said, "Nobody's there, but do you want to leave a message?"

I didn't get it and she caught my look. She reached behind her head and slid a wall picture to one side. There, built in, was a tape recorder with half-filled spools. "Cuts in after the tenth ring," she said. "Canned voice asks for a message and you're free to talk for three minutes. Besides, they record all outgoing calls. Shall I leave a message?"

"Clever," I said. "So tell her I'll be there for supper at six." I heard the flat enunciation of the canned secretary, then the message was passed on.

When she hung up the redhead said, "Tell me, Mr. . . ."

"Ryan."

". . . Mr. Ryan . . . you're not going to hurt . . . Miss Smith, are you?"

"I don't get it."

"She has lights in her eyes."

I waited for the rest of it.

She said, "I know who you are, Mr. Ryan. Although the pictures in the papers hardly flatter you."

I could feel myself go warm with a flash that only fear can start. Like a jerk I left myself wide open and this kid could put a damper on the whole thing. Maybe she saw what I was thinking. It should have been plain enough.

She smiled again. There was no malice, no guile in it at all. "I'm concerned about Miss Smith. Does she know?"

"She knows. She's helping out."

"You didn't do those things?"

"Some of them," I told her without hesitating. "They were justified. I think in the end it'll all come out clean."

"Think?"

"If I get knocked there'll be no washday, sugar. I'll be all dirty socks and bad memories, no wash, just a burial like skunk-sprayed clothes."

For a short space the laughter left her eyes and she said seriously, "Don't let that happen, Mr. Ryan."

"I'll try not to," I grinned.

There were some packages Carmen had left there and I took them with me. In their own way they provided a good cover on the street. A guy with packages has a normal look about him.

By the time I reached Carmen's apartment it was a quarter to six and I took the back way in. I got off the service elevator and used the key she had given me. When the door opened some crazy low-beat jazz flowed out at me and I saw her dancing to it in the middle of the room.

I put the packages down, walked in and watched her. She was great. To that jangled sound she danced a sensuous dance that didn't match the beat, but fitted the mood perfectly. Her sweater was tight and black and her breasts were free beneath it. Under their lovely swelling the mesh stretched and the flesh tints made startling contrasts against the black. The skirt was a full thing, deeply maroon, and when she spun it mushroomed out, giving a brief glimpse of long legs, beautifully rounded. Very deliberately, almost professionally, she twisted fast, and the mushroom flattened for a single moment and you knew that like with the sweater, there was nothing else at all. She laughed at me across the room and I caught at the studded belt she wore and drew her convexly against me and tasted her mouth.

Her breathing was deep and fast and there was a bloom in her face. Her eyes were lit up like stars and she touched my cheeks with her fingers. "I've never felt like this before, Irish."

"I haven't, either."

"I wish this were . . . for real. That we weren't . . . looking for anyone."

"We'll do it again. Another time."

"All right. Shall we eat? I have steak."

"I want you."

"Later," she said.

You got to see these places to believe them. It was what somebody had done to an old building to get floor space in one room and at the far end built a platform for the band. The johns were on either side, but you could smell them when you came in. Later, with sweat, gin and cheap perfume you wouldn't notice it, but early, they stank.

The guy at the door took the ticket and gave Carmen a double take. She went all the way with the act even to a mouthful of gum and a shoulder strap bag that was nothing more than a weapon. The robbers inside hadn't started up-pricing the soft drinks yet, waiting for the whiskey crowd to come in. All five pieces of the band were there, real gone already in a cloud of smoke. They were doing a soft cha-cha with closed eyes, not playing for anybody but themselves as yet.

I took Carmen into the dance, playing it snug right in front of the sax man. He winked down at us and let it moan low. In back of us, at the door, they were coming in fast, about three stags to every couple. It was a trouble night.

Saturday, rain, not enough dames.

I said, "You need any prompting?"

Her hair swirled to the tempo of the music. "I know what to say."

"Tell me."

"Alfredo Lias. Off the *Gastry*. I gave him money to buy me a watch overseas. He said he'd meet me here."

"And watch out for the wolves."

"I like wolves," she said.

At 10 the place was crowded. Only stragglers were still coming in. All sides of the room were lined with the stags, eyeing the women, cutting in on those they picked out. Roaming around like restless dogs were a half dozen big ones, stopping the fights that started and getting rid of the troublemakers.

I took Carmen to the soft drink concession and bought two ginger ales for a buck. Before she finished hers, a sleek-looking gook in sharp duds came over and without looking at me, asked her to dance. She glanced at me for confirmation and I said, "Go ahead, it'll be a rare experience."

The gook's face pulled tight, but he took her arm without speaking and melted into the crowd on the floor. The little guy tapped my arm and said, "Señor, be careful of that one. He did not come here just to listen to the music."

I waited until they came around again and when the gook protested, I poked my finger in his eyeball and we walked away. In back the guy screamed into his hands.

We asked around and neither of us found the one we were looking for. At midnight they drew for the door prize and some dame won a bottle of Scotch.

At one the band was looking at their watches and two good-sized fights had broken out across the room. The bouncers took care of them in a hurry and a few were hustled out lengthwise. Couples had started to leave and even the ranks of the stags were thinning out. If Lias knew his friend was dead it wasn't likely that he'd be in a gay mood. If he were anywhere he'd be on the fringe of the crowd, taking advantage of numbers.

I sent Carmen into the ladies' john to see what she could find and began to tour the stags. Most of them were in bunches, talking, arguing, drinking and all the while thinking they were having a good time. I went all around the room without seeing anyone I'd tag as Lias, then I stopped for a Coke again. Carmen had been gone quite a while and I searched for her in the crowd, trying to pick her out of the mess. The guy with the apron full of money said, "You lose your gorl, señor?"

Without thinking I said, "No . . . my friend. Afredo Lias. He's off the *Gastry*."

" 'Fredo? He was just here. He walk right behind you with that Maria." He stood on his toes and craned his neck, then shot his finger out. "See him, there he is, señor!"

I pretended to look, missing the direction. The guy said, "There, señor, the grey suit, by the empty soda boxes."

"I see him. Thanks."

"Sure, señor."

I crossed the floor, picking my way through the couples who were applauding the band. I looked at the sax man taking a bow and Carmen grabbed my arm. I pushed her ahead of me weaving through the groups.

"Ryan . . . he's here! A girl said he's with Maria and . . ."

"I know it, kid. There he is right there." I pointed to him and just then the band started another cha-cha-cha. I folded her into my arms and danced toward the one called 'Fredo. Before I reached him he stepped out onto the floor with the pretty blackhaired girl and began to lose himself in the maze.

But he didn't lose me. I steered Carmen closer and then there he was, looking down at the girl Maria without really seeing her at all. His face was a mask that hid another face that was pure terror.

We moved in close until I was standing beside him. I said, " 'Fredo . . ." and the white of fear blanched the tan of his face and when his eyes met mine they were sick to death.

I made with a laugh, old friends meeting again, forced a handshake on him and herded us all outside the dance square. I told Carmen to take Maria and powder their noses while we said hello and when they left put my arm around the guy and for everyone's benefit who wanted to look did a palsy bit that went over all the way.

But not with Alfredo Lias. His eyes came up to mine, deep and black. For some time now he had been living with this and now he thought it was here.

"You will keel me now, señor?"

I talked through a laugh and motionless lips. He was the only one who heard it. "I want you out of this mess, mister. I'm the only chance you got to get out, understand?"

He didn't but he said, "Si!"

"First we got to talk. You been here before?"

"Si. Often we come here."

"Anything out back? We have to talk somewhere."

His hand was like a talon around my forearm, hope giving him new life again. "By the corner is a door. Out back is where the garbage is put. Señor, they will kill me, no?"

"I hope not, kiddo. You go back there. I'll tell the girls to stay put and cruise on out."

"Si! I go. I tell you anything."

He walked away and angled across the dance floor. I waited beside the johns until Carmen and Maria came out then told them to hang on. Neither asked any questions. They seemed glad to talk.

I cut across in front of the bandstand where they started the next number. Halfway across I stopped and stared at the guy dancing with the tall, raven-haired doll. I said, "Hi, kid."

Jake McGaffney looked at me and said, "What're you doing here, Irish?"

"What about you?"

He grinned at the doll. "Hell, ask Bets here. She drags me to all these damn native affairs."

The doll smiled, said something to me in Spanish and danced off with Jake.

I got across to the other side, behind two kids wheeling out cardboard containers of refuse. The first one pulled at the door and while it was all the way open the night was split apart by the slamming reverberations of three close shots and right behind it every girl in the place began to scream her lungs out.

There was one mad rush for the front exits and curses spit out in a dozen different languages. Up front they clawed their way to the street over one another, knowing full well what those blasts meant. The two kids had jumped off like startled rabbits leaving the container wedged in the doorway and I had to climb over it to get outside.

My hand was tight around the butt of the .45 and I sucked myself into the shadows. I waited a full minute, but it didn't matter at all. Whoever fired the shots had gone.

But I wasn't alone. The small sound came from behind the stacked soda crates and I saw the dull grey of his suit and the contrasting brown of his face. He was almost white now. He had one hand across his stomach and he had no reason to be alive at all.

I knelt beside him, the gun still in my hand. He saw it, but I shook my head. "I didn't do it, 'Fredo."

His voice was a harsh whisper. "I know . . . señor."

"Did you see him?"

"No. He was . . . behind me. I thought . . . it was you."

"Look, I'll get you a doctor . . ."

His hand touched my arm. "Señor . . . please, no. It is too late. I get bad. Now I pay. Like Tom. I pay. It is better."

I didn't argue with him. I said, "You know what you took from the ship?"

He nodded, his eyes half closed.

"What was it, 'Fredo?"

A hiccup caught at his chest and I knew there were only seconds left. "Eight . . . kilos . . . señor," he whispered.

Then I knew what it was all about. I wanted one last confirmation. " 'Fredo . . . listen. Juan talked you into selling to Billings?" His nod was weak and his eyes closed. "Somehow you heard about Lodo. All of you knew about Lodo?"

I put my ear close to his mouth. "We . . . are all . . . dead men . . . señor."

"Billings had the eight kilos last then?"

Another whisper. "Si."

" 'Fredo . . . who is Lodo?"

There was nothing more he could say.

From outside you could hear the sirens and the voices, and more sirens and more voices. They were getting louder and I couldn't wait. I went over the fence the way the killer had gone and like the way a city-bred animal can, found my way back to the open street and the safety of the night and the rain.

I had to show the cabbie the money before he'd take me back. He let me off where I asked and I found Pete-the-Dog selling his papers on the ginmill beat. I took him outside, bought all of his sheets for a couple minutes talk and got what I wanted. Some unknowns had brought action into the block. Somebody shilled Golden into popping off and he was dead. Holmes was in an emergency ward with a couple of slugs in his chest and not expected to live. Steckler was picked up on an assault charge against Razztazz and to top it a Sullivan Act violation which kicked his parole out and he was due in the big house for the rest of his stretch. Razz was okay. A little beat, but okay. I gave Pete his papers back and started back to the house.

The womb.

The familiar pattern, I thought. That's all a hood had was his house. His womb. You die in sleep. Each awakening was a birth. It was something precious, something you couldn't take away.

There hadn't been time to find Carmen, but I knew, somehow, that she'd be all right. Tomorrow I'd see her. Tomorrow.

I walked down the street paying no attention to the rain at all. It slashed down at me, the wind giving it a sharp bite. I held my head up and let it lick at my face. The stinging sensation had a cleansing, astringent effect and I thought over all the things that had happened. Not just tonight. All the other nights. There didn't have to be any more looking because I knew I had all the pieces. They were there. They would just take a little sorting out in the morning and I'd have the whole picture. Then the money. Then Carmen. Then life.

I opened my coat, held the .45 in my hand while I fumbled my key out. I shouldn't've bothered because the door was already open. I took my hat off, held it while I felt my way to the living room and flipped on the switch.

Even before the first blossom of light filled the room

I remembered what was wrong. Pete-the-Dog hadn't mentioned one name, Mario Sen.

And here he was waiting for me to come in the door and his gun was leveled right at my stomach. He waited to let me see him smile his killer's smile and it was a smile too long. He never noticed the .45 in my fist under the hat I was holding and my first slug blew his brains all over the wall. The cordite and blood stink rushed into the room and for the first time I felt a little sick.

Out in the kitchen I let the water run until it was cold, took a long drink to wash the bitterness away that stained my mouth and went to the phone. I dialed the Big Man's number and when he came on I said, "This is Ryan. I found Lias. He's dead."

"I heard the report."

"He wasn't dead when I reached him, Big Man."

The intake of his breath made a sharp hiss. "What was it?"

"Big Man . . . about how much would eight kilos of heroin be worth on the final cut?"

He tried to keep the excitement out of his voice but couldn't make it. "That's way up in the millions. There hasn't been a single shipment that size in twenty years!"

"That's what was in your package, mister. That's why everybody died."

"Have you located it?"

"Not yet. But I will. If you had a tail on Billings all the while, where did he hang around?"

"Hold on."

I heard a file drawer slide open, the rustle of papers, then the drawer slam shut. He picked up the phone again. "His movements were pretty well regimented. Mornings at the Barkley for breakfast and a shave, on to the Green Bow or Nelson's, several bars in the Forties and generally into the Snyder House for a card game at night. Just before he was killed he made two trips to where the city's planning that new Valley Park Housing Development. Walked around the block, but that was all."

"Those buildings are going to be torn down," I said.

"In a few months. There are still some families there yet."

"I know," I said.

"Any help?"

"Yes. Yes. Lots of help. Meantime you can pick up another dead man at my place. His name is Mario Sen.

He won't be missed. He was planted here to get me and you guys passed him over. I took care of it myself." I paused, then added, "I'll call you back."

I hung up the phone while he was still trying to talk and sat down. It made lots of sense now. I knew what Billings was doing in that old section. I had an apartment there for 10 years and he found out where. He was going to plant the stuff in my pad before he died and let it go from there.

The only thing he didn't know was that I had just moved out!

I reached for the phone again, held my hand on it and thought back, all the way back to the beginning and ran it up to date. There was no more puzzle then. The pieces became a picture and faces and times and events and now there was nothing left to find out at all . . . except for one thing.

All the tiredness left me and I felt good again, like that day in the beginning. The sucker trap was over and I was out of it and after tonight there wouldn't be a kill list at all. Not for me. For a lot of others, maybe, but not me.

I grabbed at the phone, rang Carmen's number and she had it before it finished ringing the first time. Her voice almost cracked with anxiety when she said, "Ryan, Ryan, where are you?"

"Home, Baby, I'm okay. What happened?"

"We left with the rest. The police came up as I came out but there weren't enough to catch us. We heard those shots and I thought it was you. I couldn't get over there. It was like being caught in the tide. Everybody was screaming and pressing forward . . ."

"You can forget it now."

"Who was it?"

" 'Fredo. They got him."

"Oh, Ryan."

"He was alive when I got there. He talked, kitten, and now I can really twist some tails. You want to see it happen?"

"Only . . . if I can help."

"You can. Look, grab a cab and come over here, I'll be waiting outside. We can go on from here." I gave her my address, hung up and went in and changed my shirt. I walked past Mario Sen to the street and stood in the shadows, waiting.

When the cab stopped I got in and there was my lovely

Carmen. Her breath half-caught in a relieved sob. She said my name and buried her face against my neck. I gave the driver my old address.

The street was dying. What life it had left showed in the few windows glowing a sickly yellow. Only a handful of kids made noises under the street lights. The plague it had even seemed to reroute traffic which hurried by as if anxious to get away from the old and decaying.

I stopped, and Carmen looked up at me quizzically, her hand tight on my arm. "Thinking?"

"Reliving a little."

"Oh?"

"I used to live here." I nodded toward the blank row of windows that faced the second floor.

A thin stoop-shouldered old man, his face gaunt under the grey velvet of a beard, shuffled out of the darkness, glanced at us suspiciously, then twisted his mouth into a grin. "Evenin', Mr. Ryan. You come back for a last look?"

"Hi, Sandy. No, just a little unfinished business. How come you're still here?"

"That Kopek Wrecking outfit got a bunch of us around. Supposed to keep out sleepers. You remember when they knocked down that place with them two bums holed up inside? Cost them for that."

I motioned toward the hallway on my right. "Anybody here?"

"Steve. He'll be drunk. You want to see him?"

"Not specially."

He flipped an off beat salute and said, "Well, have fun. Can't see why anybody'd come back here. Three more weeks everybody's out and down they come."

We watched him walk off and Carmen said, "Sad little man."

I took her arm and we went up the time worn brownstone steps into the open maw of the tenement.

The scars of occupancy were still fresh, the *feel* of people still there. The pale light of the unshaded bulb overhead gave a false warmth and cast long, strange shadows around us. From somewhere in the back came a cough and the mumble of a voice thick with liquor.

A box-like professional torch with *Kopek Wrecking* stenciled on it was wedged in the angle between the bannister and the newel post. I picked it up and snapped on the switch. Then I smiled at Carmen, took her hand and started up the stairs.

At the door I stopped and turned her head toward mine. "You haven't said anything."

Her eyes laughed at me. She waved her hand at the darkness outside the light. "What can I say? Everything is so . . . strange." An involuntary shiver seemed to touch her and she drew closer to me. "The things you do . . . are so different. I never know what to expect."

"They're hood things, kitten."

For a moment she seemed pensive, then she shook her head lightly. "You're not really, Ryan. In the beginning you were, but something's happened to you."

"Not to me, sugar. Nothing in this whole lousy world is going to shake me up. I like being a hood. To me it's the only way I can tell off this stupid race of slobs. I can keep out of their damned organizations and petty grievances and keep them away from me. I can drink my own kind of poison and be dirty mean when they want me to drink theirs."

I tried the knob. It turned easily and the door opened. In a way it was like visiting your own tomb.

There was my chair by the window. The dropleaf table Mrs. Winkler gave me was still in its usual position by the wall. Somebody had stolen the mirror and the magazine rack. When I turned the light into the bedroom the framework of the iron bed made a grilled pattern in shadows on the wall. Somebody had swiped the mattresses too.

I walked to the window and looked out into the street. The haze of dirt put things out of focus. I turned the head of the torch ceilingwise and put it on the floor, then sat down in the armchair.

Almost softly I said, "It's a 'once-upon-a-time' story. It started in Lisbon where two drunks named 'Fredo and Spanish Tom accidentally witnessed the caching of a narcotics shipment. In cubic displacement it only made a small package, eight kilos worth, but in value a multimillion dollar proposition. They never realized the full value of it. A few grand was as far as they could think.

"But others knew what it meant. In port they contacted a Spanish speaking buddy, Juan Gonzales. He knew a guy who had the loot to make the buy. That takes us to my old friend Billings. The louse."

For some reason I didn't feel the quick flush of hate I used to feel when I thought of his name.

"Juan made the buy for Billings, all right, and probably before he could pass over the ten grand he paid for it to Tom and 'Fredo, they shipped out. Juan didn't care for ten grand . . . you see, he was going to be Billings' partner in something really *big*. He even told his wife the great things they'd do . . . things you don't do on only ten grand.

"And now the rub. Billings didn't want a partner. The big cross was coming up and Juan could feel it. He didn't have a chance in the world and he protected his wife the only way he could. He gave her that ten grand then tried to skip out. He didn't get far. Billings was waiting. He shoved him under a truck and that took care of Juan. He didn't worry about the other two since they never knew who made the buy."

The curiosity in her eyes deepened. Her tongue made a slight movement between her teeth as she followed my thought. She said, "But those other two . . . they're dead."

"I know. I'll come to that."

"Billings put eight kilos of junk on the market. I can't figure how he could have been so incredibly stupid, but apparently his greed got the better of him. *Eight kilos!* This was the biggest load that ever hit the States in one piece!"

I stopped a moment, thought about it, then said reflectively, "You know, this was what they were waiting for."

"They?" She was perched on the edge of the dropleaf table, her hands folded under her breasts making them strain against the fabric of the raincoat.

"*They*, sugar. Whenever eight kilos of H gets away from its handlers there's some hell waiting for somebody. An organizational hijacking they could cope with, but not coincidence. They didn't know where it was, but they knew it would show up in time. When it did they went after it and Billings was their target. The slob got smart too late.

"When the word went out how hot the junk was nobody would touch it. There were no buyers. That's when Billings knew he was about to be tapped. He tried to protect himself by going to a policing agency, but again it was too late. The stakes were too high. They knocked off his protection, moved in close and were ready to tap him out.

"Buddy Billings made his final move. He knew they wanted the stuff as well as him, so like he had done once before, he included me in the mess. Hell, he knew where I lived. He wanted me dead or imprisoned . . .

anything to pay for the anxiety I had made him live with all the days I had hunted for him."

I stopped, sucked in a deep breath and looked at the ceiling patterns again.

"He hid the junk in my place, kid. He probably figured on writing an anonymous letter or something but they caught up with him beforehand. He wasn't quite dead when a cop found him. His last words implicated me.

"Now catch this. By now the underworld has been rattling with this story. The policy agency involved have a good picture of what they're after. This stuff has to be found before the original owners get it and put it into circulation.

"The catch, kiddo. They have two names. Mine, and a certain Lodo. The last one is a killer. The head of operation kill. The wheel that Mafia HQ keeps set up to enforce its East Coast programs and keep things in line. Lodo is rarely called upon, that's how clever the organization is, how big it is, how tightly it can work within the frameworks of certain governments. Narcotics are big . . . and legal . . . businesses in several countries. Lodo is an important cog in the machine . . . and Lodo is only a cover name.

"Lodo must be smart, untouchable, able to operate without suspicion. And now Lodo is responsible for recovery of eight kilos of H."

She began to see what I was driving at. "And all that time it was . . . at your place?"

"That's right."

She looked around quickly. "Here?"

I nodded. "Billings' mistake. He didn't know about the move."

"All that . . . is here?"

"I could almost say where."

She waited, her face reflecting her interest. I got up, went to the kitchen and in the barren limits of the light felt for the obvious wall partition by the sink that opened onto a series of valves. I hauled the carton out and shut the partition. My arm hit a cup that still stood on the sink and it crashed to the floor.

In the living room I heard Carmen gasp.

I put the carton beside the torch and sat down. "There was no other place in this dump to hide anything," I said.

The box fascinated her. I tapped it with my foot. "Eight

kilos. Millions. Not one or two. Not ten. More than that. Enough to get a whole city killed off."

"It . . . doesn't seem like much," she admitted.

"It never does."

"And you found it. Nobody else could. Just you." Her voice held a touch of admiration and she was smiling.

"There were red herrings. Money Billings won on the nags. The fuzz thought it was loot I paid him for the stuff. *You know, all that time they sucked me in thinking I had possession and were trying to get it out of me. They knew I had to play their little game or else.*"

"Game?"

"Sure, sweetie. In my own crazy way I'm a fuzz too. They played the game to the hilt. They played it two ways at once and played it smart. I was the complete unknown and they didn't know what to do with me. What they pulled might be called the Ultimate Stunt. I like that. It fits real well. But what I like best is what I told them in the beginning. I was right. I was bigger than their whole damn department. Hoodtown's my back yard too and the game is my game as much as theirs. If I felt like it I could bust this play open like a ripe egg. Alone."

I said suddenly, "What made you do it, Carmen?"

She frowned and asked the question silently.

"Take the job, I mean."

"Job?"

"*Lodo,*" I said softly. *"My beautiful big lovely is Lodo."*

Her breath came in a gasp. "Ryan!"

"I'm going to guess again, kid. Check me. You probably never have before. But look deep. Look at a kid brought up around the gaming tables whose ears catch talk and intents kids shouldn't hear. Look at a kid who gets used to wrong money young, who learns the mechanics of card handling from an expert and who finds a taste for those things develops into a lust for them."

The next thing I let come out slowly.

"Look at a kid who blew a guy's head off from ten feet away and think of what impact that had on a mind already decaying."

For a moment a terrible shudder touched her shoulders and the beauty of her face was twisted with anguish.

"Stop it, Ryan! These things you're guessing . . ."

I shook my head. "I'm not guessing any more, kitten."

Her teeth bit into her lip and the tears that made her eyes swim flooded out and coursed down her cheeks.

I said, "Lodo left a line to Billings . . . a slim one, a

deliberate one. Lodo had to maintain that connection to be in on things if they ever developed, yet not enough to be suspicious. That line was the sweet bouquet you sent the departed. The eventuality paid off. *I* followed it.

"Your next move was easy. On our first lunch date you went to the ladies room as per usual, but made a phone call that had me tailed. You made all the provisions for a tap job in my own apartment using organization punks and sat back and waited."

"Ryan . . ." her eyes were pleading, "do you think I *could* do that?"

"Sure. The kill wasn't yours directly. You just made the call. Operation tappo went into effect automatically. Trouble was, it didn't come off. The big second phase began. I was cultivated for information. I was still an enigma. Nobody could figure my part in it at all. Hell, don't feel sorry about it, I didn't either."

She shook her head, telling me it was wrong, all wrong, but I didn't watch.

"My friend Art died before I could catch on. He had some great connections, that guy. They went pretty far. He was a big hero in the Italian campaign during the war. He made a lot of friends over there. He called on one to do some poking for him. He found out Lodo was a cover name and was about to find out who Lodo was. So Art had to die.

"Coincidence entered the picture again. You weren't deliberately set up for it . . . the gimmick was just there, that's all."

"Gimmick?" Her voice was quiet, her face expressionless.

"The tape recorder attachment on the phone. One in the office, one at home. You picked up my conversation with Art, went to his place and while he was asleep, killed him yourself or had him killed."

"No!"

I shrugged. "It really doesn't matter who did it. I prefer thinking it was you. By this time your organization had run down the Lisbon kids. One was bumped, one to go. The game was all yours when I figured when the last one would be. You had your stooges there and waiting and when the contact was made they beat me to the guy and the tap cleaned up that end of things."

I leaned back in the chair and stretched out my feet. "Pretty quick now this outfit of yours will take plenty of lumps."

"Please, Ryan . . ."

"You suckered me, kiddo. I'm sore at the whole business now. I'm sore because when things were getting tight you called out the troops. I was on everybody's kill list. All the big ones were called in, guns from all over the country. Suddenly I'm thinking like fuzz and want the whole damn bunch slammed. Suddenly I know that for a change I can be useful. Suddenly I see that playing hood isn't the big thing after all because it's playing with the things I hate."

I took a big, deep breath. "And suddenly I'm hating those things especially hard because I started to be in love for the first time and now I don't know if it will ever happen again. Suddenly I have a terrible feeling like when I walked in the room here. It's all over. Everything's all over. The mistakes have all been made and now it's all over."

And then she showed me how the first part was wrong and the second right. The mistake still to go was mine in thinking I could get my rod out before she could move. I was wrong. It was about to be all over. In that I was right.

I could see the hole in the end of the hammerless automatic she pointed at my head. It was a fascinating thing, a bottomless black eye. I looked over it at Carmen's smile. It was strained at first, then relaxed.

She was still very beautiful.

"What would you have done, Ryan?"

I shrugged, gauging the distance between us. I'd make the try, all right, but it would be no use.

"You were right, you know." She tossed her head, making her hair swirl again. "The Peter Haynes Company is a front. Very legal, economically sound. A wonderful place to keep . . . other records. A good source of income to keep key personnel in funds and in style until their services are needed. My file of personal correspondence there would be very enlightening to a cipher expert, but completely meaningless to anyone else."

When I gave her a hard smile she said, "That one little fact could break and smash half of the whole organization."

And now it was too late.

"What would you have done, Ryan?"

"I don't know."

"Killed me?"

I didn't lie about it. "No."

"Being a hood never became you. The one act of turning me in would have justified you. You could have walked straight again. I think now you really want to.

"Two things would have happened. In this state, the chair . . . or with a good lawyer, permanently confined to a mental institution. I couldn't live that way. It would be better to be dead."

Her face softened and the light glinted on the wetness that lay along her cheeks. "Only you couldn't kill me, Ryan. Why?"

"What difference does it make?"

I could hardly make out her words. "It makes a difference."

"I told you. I was falling in love. I was a jerk. So now I pay for being a jerk. A whole lifetime I laugh at the idiots who get tied up in love knots and then it happens to me. Well at least I won't be hurting for long. I'm going to make you do it to me fast, kitten."

"Please don't." Her lip was tight in her teeth, choking something back. "Did you really love me, Irish?"

"Okay, kid, get the last laugh. Make it loud. It was true. You were the one. I loved you very much."

Inside my heart was slamming against my ribs because I knew it was coming and I didn't know whether it would hurt or not and I was scared. I looked at her and tried to see inside her mind but I couldn't get past the tears. For some reason she smiled and it was like before when I didn't know all the things I did now and when I could look at her and want and hope. Her eyes were soft and misty and in their depths saw what happened to her . . . saw the realization come, the analysis, the rejection of the future and the decision. I saw her suddenly love and give the only thing she had to give and with the yell still choked in my throat and before I could move to stop her she said, "I love you, man."

Then she folded her arms and turned the gun against her heart and said the same words again only this time they were shattered by the blast of the gunshot.

RETURN
OF THE HOOD

Chapter 1

NEWBOLDER and Schmidt were decent about it. They came in, nodded and sat down at their table with coffee in front of them and let me alone to finish my supper. Sometimes you just can't figure cops. But once they made their touch, there was no sense running. Try it and you can get shot down. Go along with the game and you have a chance. Besides, the Cafeteria was a popular place and the owner a swell egg who didn't deserve getting shook by a big punch right in the middle of his rush hour.

So I nodded back and let them know I was ready when I cleaned my plate and that there wouldn't be any fireworks or tough talk no matter how big the beef was. And it was a big beef. Real big. I was a murder suspect and in a way it was lucky the cops made the scene first because in the same neighborhood the Stipetto brothers were canvassing the area for me too and with them it meant playing guns.

With them I could play. I had a .45 calibre instrument that could sound off loud and clear, but with cops you don't play like that. On somebody else the fuzz would have stepped up and made the pinch without waiting. For this one time I had to be an exception because of what happened a year ago, and for that they were being decent. Something like General Arnold's boot if you got enough smarts to know what I mean.

The cops didn't watch me. I was there, part of their peripheral vision, they weren't in any hurry at all and were glad to sit in out of the rain and the cold for a few minutes. They had the faces of cops all over the world that you can't miss if you're in the business on one side or the other.

Across the room with his back to the wall, Wally Pee who ran numbers for Sal Upsidion started to sweat and couldn't finish what was on his tray. He kept glancing from Newbolder and Schmidt to Izzy Goldwitz, who was at the counter getting seconds, because Izzy had six grand in cash in the overnight bag he carried and with Sal Upsidion you didn't give any excuses if it didn't get turned in. When Izzy paid the cashier and started back he caught Wally's signal and turned white, but by then it was too late to do anything except finish supper, so he sat down and tried to bluff it out.

I could have gone over and told them, but it didn't make any difference anyway and for them it was better to sweat a little so that the next time they'd be on their toes more. Newbolder's quick case of the place didn't make them since I was his target and not much else mattered, so the numbers boys were off the hook for this time, anyway.

Funny, funny.

New York after dark, a vivid chameleon who by day was a roaring scaly dragon of business and ceremony, and by night a soft quivering thing because the guts of the city had gone home leaving the shell to be invaded by parasites.

The few who stayed, and the tourists, kept to the Gay White Way as they used to name it, clubbing, bar hopping or taking in a show. But the perimeter of life had closed down to the very heart of the city. Beyond the perimeter was where the dying came. A few arteries of light and life extended crosstown, went up a ways and down a ways, but that was all. The great verdant cancer of Central Park was like a sparkling jewel, laced with the multicolor of taxis whose beams probed ahead of them with twin fingers, always searching. Like Damocles.

Around me the restaurant was packed with people from Jersey, Brooklyn, the Island, all getting ready to go home or take in the town a little. The regulars were there too, the handful of natives whose home was Manhattan no matter what. Some were night people like me and Wally Pee and Izzy; the others came because the food was good and inexpensive.

I wondered what my chances were on the rap. They didn't look good at all.

Somebody had knocked off Penny Stipetto. Two days before I had belted his ass from one end of 45th and Second all the way to the next corner for shaking down Rudy Max and when he healed up he strapped on a rod and went looking for me with a skinful of big H to keep his courage up.

Word travels fast in this town. I got the news and passed it back that I was ready and available any time, any place and if I saw him first he was going to get laid out.

Trouble was, I didn't see him first.

Somebody else did and they found Penny Stipetto wedged behind a couple of garbage cans two blocks away from my pad with a hole in his head.

That was enough for the remaining brothers Stipetto. They spread out a net across the city that was as efficient as any the fuzz could throw and pulled the strings tight until I only had one block to run in and one place to go.

The condemned man ate a hearty meal.

Hell, I was *glad* Newbolder and Schmidt found me first. This was the age of enlightened crime and a gang shoot-out comes only of immediate necessity. Revenge is a thing of the past except for the extreme occasion, and if the law will do the job equally as well, then let it go, man. In fact, the brothers Stipetto would only be too happy to help the fuzz nail my hide. They'd make damn sure *somebody* saw me in the area at the time Penny took the big slide and damn sure any alibi I had would fold if they had to remove it forever.

In other words, I was a dead duck. I had no alibi to begin with unless a warm solo pad could be called one, the hole in Penny's head was big enough to be made by at least a .45 and no spent slug was recovered for comparison. I had the motive, the time, a probable weapon and on top of it all, the critical, anti-social personality that, according to the psycho meds, made such a deed possible.

In short, I was a hood.

Newbolder sipped his coffee and glanced at his watch. He wasn't rushing me, but I knew he'd like to get off his shift on time and a cop can only be decent so long. By then Wally Pee and Izzy Goldswitz had caught the pitch and were begging me with their eyes to get the hell out before the cops decided to case the place for any other interesting characters and spotted them.

Let them take care of themselves, I thought, and went back to the Hungarian goulash. It was good and there was no telling when I'd be getting another plate of the stuff.

I had almost finished when the broad sat down. Like they'll always do, she sat down directly opposite me rather than at the side, trying to make out as if she had the table all to herself. I knew she was an out-of-towner when she ate without taking the dishes off her tray, something a cafeteria regular never would do.

There was something odd about her I couldn't place, but in New York you don't stare too long or take deliberate second looks because privacy is a funny thing, like the props in theatre-in-the-round. Privacy exists because you pretend nothing else is there and in a chow joint you're expected to obey the rules of the game.

But I couldn't help the second look. I made it as surreptitious as possible and found the flaw. The tall girl with the deep chestnut hair was made up to perfection, if perfection meant deliberately disguising a classic beauty to become just another fairly pretty dame worth smiling at sometimes, but not much more.

They do that sometimes. Broads get screwy ideas about their looks and plenty of times I've seen real treats done up in trick suits in the beatnik shops.

Who are you today, honey—Hepburn? You could be LaMarr if you liked. You have a luscious mouth with the kind of pouty lips that can kiss like crazy but the lipstick is wrong. That eyebrow pencil accent is way off too. Way off. And you can't quite erase genes that put a tricky, exotic slant in your eyes and cheekbones with cleverly applied green shadows and too-pale makeup.

When she shrugged the white trench coat off, I saw it was only her face that had been changed to the mediocre. Nothing could have been done to alter the magnificence of her body. There was just too much of her, just too much big, lovely much.

The condemned man ate a hearty meal. Visually, that is.

So while they waited for me, those outside watching to make sure those inside didn't slip, I feasted a little bit and knew I was wearing a crooked grin that couldn't be helped but could be hidden if I chewed hard enough.

Newbolder had shifted his seat a little so he could see around the broad, not giving up his cop's habits for any reason, and I finished my goulash and started in on my pie.

It was just a voice. It was strangely low, detached and was there without seeming to come from any one point. It was almost totally lost in the grand hum of voices that kept the room in motion and for a second I couldn't place it.

When I did I kept on eating, doing a quick think because it was the broad speaking to me con style without moving her lips or changing her expression, and all the while managing to eat as if she were completely alone.

"Can you talk without looking at me?"

In my racket you learn to play by ear real fast or get

dead real fast and I had nothing to lose at all any more.

So I said, "Go ahead, honey," and like her, my mouth didn't move either except to eat.

The broad caught it immediately and said, "You did time?" and there was a hesitancy in her voice.

"No. Not quite. The fuzz would like me to go down though."

"Service record?"

That was a peculiar angle for a new line to take. I was trying to figure her for a high class hooker or a tomato with a hot item for sale, but this bit threw the picture out of focus. I did a mental shrug and said, "A whole war, kid, but that was twenty years ago." I half-laughed and smothered it. "Even got a few medals out of it."

"I'm in trouble."

"It figures," I said.

She buttered a piece of roll, bit off a bite and glanced vacantly around the room. I cut into my pie with my fork and concentrated on my last meal.

"You'll have to help," she finally got out.

I swallowed and forked out another bit of pie. "Why?"

"You're the only one who looks capable."

"Of what?"

She lifted her coffee cup and sipped at it. "Killing somebody if you have to."

This time it wasn't so easy to swallow the pie. I kept chewing, wondering why the hell I always drew the loonies. Sooner or later they always wind up in my lap. "Come off it, baby," I told her softly.

She didn't try to argue about it. She made it a square, simple statement that put her either way out or close inside and left me right in the middle no matter what happened.

She said, "My name is Karen Sinclair. I'm a government agent working with *Operation Hightower*. In my mouth I have a capsule containing a strip of microfilm that must be delivered to the head of our bureau at once. It's a matter of national safety. *Is that clear? National security is involved.* I'm going to bite into a roll, push it inside and put the rest of the roll down. When I leave you pick that roll up and get it in the hands of the nearest F.B.I. agent. Can you do that?"

"Sure." It was all I could think of to say. It still wasn't making sense. Finally, I added, "What's the act for?"

Unconcernedly, she said, "Because outside there are

three men who are going to kill me to get that capsule back and we can't let it happen."

I was almost done with my pie and couldn't stall much longer. Newbolder and Schmidt were getting impatient. "More, baby."

With an involuntary gesture, she bit her lip, remembered in time to fake it and sipped at her coffee again. "They were almost ready to take me on the street. They know I have no contact here and am headed for a certain point so they suppose I really stopped to eat. What they don't realize is that I spotted them."

"Look, if you're serious. . . ."

"I'm serious." Her voice was the same flat monotone, yet had a new note to it, quiet and deadly. She wasn't lying.

"Hell, girl, I can . . ."

"You can do nothing, mister. If you want to help do as you're told. That's the only way this information can be passed on to the right people. You're the only chance I have. I know what I'm up against. I've been in this game a long time too and knew the odds when I started. I hate to have to pass this to amateurs but when I picked you it was because you had all the signs of the kind of man who can live outside the law and still hang on to certain principles. I hope I'm right."

She picked up a roll, broke it in half and nibbled into it. What she did, she did quickly, putting the remainder of the roll back on the plate, then washing it down with the rest of her coffee. She finished quickly without seeming to be in a hurry, put her arms back into the trench coat, belted it and picked up her pocketbook.

Before she left I felt her eyes scan my face briefly and sensed the greenish heat of there.

"Thanks," she said, then turned and walked away.

Indifferently, I picked the half a roll up, dunked it in my coffee, and chewed into it. The capsule was a brittle plastic against my teeth and when I wiped my mouth I spit it out in my hand and quietly stuck it in my watch pocket, then finished the roll.

If it was a gag, it was a beauty.

If it wasn't, then there was big trouble happening too fast for me to think out.

Newbolder stood up and so did I. It was about that time and now I was going to have the blocks put to me but good. Both cops knew I had the .45 on me and although they knew it was there for the Stipetto crowd

they didn't take the big chance and kept their hands
held just-so right above their Police Specials. This one
time they'd play it neat all the way to the squad car for
old time's sake and after that all bets were off.

I put on my hat, picked up my coat when two shots
blew the night apart outside and a great blast tore the
window out of the restaurant and scattered fragments
all over the place. Women screamed as though they were
given a downbeat and tables overturning in the sudden
rush away from the front were like the crashing cymbals
of a mad symphony.

I saw Newbolder and Schmidt pull at their guns and
run for the door as another handful of shots were triggered off and in that one instant the door was open as
they ran through I saw the big girl falling against a car
at the curb while the gun in her hand pointed at something out of sight and spouted tiny red flashes.

The decision wasn't mine at all. She had made it for
me. I did the same thing everybody else did and ran,
letting the crowd cover me. There was only one difference. I knew where I was running. I got to the door leading to the dishwashing section, went through quickly and
paused, looking for another exit. I spotted it down the
end, took a fast look through the small window in the
door behind me and knew that it was no kind of a gag at
all. A harmless looking rabbity guy whom I had unconsciously noticed trying to come across the room against
the fleeing crowd had reached my table and was going
through the remnants around the girl's plate. He finished,
made a gesture toward where I had been sitting and
stopped, then looked around thoughtfully and followed
the crowd toward the main kitchen doors.

I would have liked it if he had come in beside me, but
he hadn't as yet. He would, but I wasn't going to wait.

Any broad that would go all the way out, even knowing
she was going to get hit, just to deliver a small package,
needed a hand up. I fingered out the capsule and looked
at it for the first time. It was transparent and inside was
a packed white powder. Clever. It could appear to be a
medicine. But there was a faint pinpoint of dark against
the plastic where a corner of hidden microfilm touched
it. I grinned, put it back in my pocket and took off for
the doorway.

It swung out into a corridor lit by a single overhead
bulb. By the exit doorway was a light switch I flicked

off so I wouldn't step out silhouetted against a bright room.

My precautions almost worked.

Almost. Not quite.

There was a funny *shock* you hear rather than feel when metal hits bone and an overwhelming stuffiness began to smother me and I knew that I hadn't made it after all.

Chapter 2

ALL RIGHT, I thought, where the hell am I now? I realized I was conscious without first experiencing sight or sound, a peculiar awareness that was common to a person coming out of a deep sleep. I lay there a moment, deliberately thoughtful, concentrating on the moment, trying to retrieve my last hours of remembrance.

They came with the physical sensation of restriction and with a sudden jolt I felt the ropes that bit into my ankles and wrists. I was sitting up, hands and legs tied to a chair, my mouth open slackly and my head hanging forward limply. For a while I stayed like that, watching my feet and thinking. Just thinking.

From behind me the girl said, "Why did you bring him here, Fly? You crazy?"

A nervous, slimey voice said, "Maybe you got a better idea? Why you think Big Step made me stay back there. He figured this guy might pull something and he sure did. That he sure did."

"Big Step didn't want him here. He wasn't going to bring him here. They was supposed to go someplace in Jersey."

"Sure they was, but who knew this punk had guns around? Outside he had two guys and a broad who started shooting up then Carl and Moe figured they was part of this guy's bunch and cut loose at 'em. Then them two cops come outa the joint and everything goes to hell, like. Man, ain't nothing like that since that business in Havana before Castro."

"I don't care," the girl insisted, "you better take him someplace else."

"Not me, Lisa, not me. You think Big Step won't want him even more now? First Penny dead, now Little Step and Carl and Moe. Big Step, he's gonna wanta carve on this here punk now for sure and whoever puts him outa reach is in for it."

"Listen, Fly, first thing the fuzz does is look around Big Step's places and that means the first thing they come here. This looks good with him here? Big Step wants a kidnapping rap besides? Maybe he can cover for the shooting . . . he woulda been somewhere else while it was going on, but this he won't hold still for."

The one called Fly pushed back a chair and walked around the room. I knew the guy. He was a cheap hood from the east side who did errands for the Stipetto brothers and lived off the white *Horse* he peddled around the neighborhood. He was his own best customer.

"So what'll I do?"

Lisa said, "Go bring up a car. We can get him over back of the store until we hear from Big Step."

Fly was glad to have somebody else make the decision. He grunted an acknowledgment, came over to me and yanked my head up. I kept my eyes closed and played it cute.

He said "You awake, Ryan? Come on, punk. Up. Wake up." He gave me a backhand across the jaw that didn't do much except make me put down another mental mark in his dead book. "Quit stallin', Ryan. You hear me?"

"Let him be," Lisa cut in. "You sapped him pretty hard."

"Damn right I did. This boy carries a big piece. You see that .45 I took off'n him?"

"I saw it," Lisa said, her tone bored.

"He had a cap of H on him too. You know that?"

This time Lisa sounded more interested. "Him? I didn't know this big coot blasted any?"

"He carried it. In his watch pocket."

"Well, he always was a nervy guy. So now we know. He's like all the rest. Got to get his nerve up a vein."

"He won't get this one. I'm running short myself and I won't have time to get to Ike South if we gotta drag him around." He let my head go and deliberately, I let it slump back down.

Now everything was screwed up proper. Real *snafu*. The one thing that broke me out of the big bind in the restaurant winds up in a hype's pocket and I'm worse off than I ever was.

Think, boy, I told myself. *Think awfully hard. Life in college those two years way back so long ago. Show your book learning. You got going against you only one scrawny doped up punk and a broad Big Stipetto kept on his side. How formidable could they be?*

Pretty formidable. Before I could think Fly swung at the back of my head and that far off sound of metal on bone, quieted by a small layer of flesh in between, reached me from far off and the black was with me again.

When sense and sound and sight came back, it flushed a searing pain down the back of my skull into my spine. It lasted a few minutes before settling down to a steady throbbing at the base of my head. This time I was on the floor, my hands behind me, my ankles tied and drawn up so they touched my fingers. In the old days they used to throw a loop around your neck too so that any movement would mean you choked yourself to death.

Fly said, "He's okay now. You okay, Ryan?"

I swore at him.

"See, I told you he was all right. I don't know why the hell you was worried about him. Big Step is only gonna knock him off anyway. Now you wait here and don't leave, you hear?"

"I'm not staying . . ."

"Maybe you'd like for me to pass that on to Big Step. He'd flatten your face agin, you give him any trouble now. Maybe nobody'll come in, but if'n they do, somebody better be here to steer 'em off."

"You hurry," Lisa sulked.

"Nuts, baby. Nobody's hurryin' Big Step. First I gotta find him. He ain't gonna be a happy one when I do. With Little Step dead he's liable to come over here running. Maybe he'll want to wait to enjoy what he's gonna do even more. You just stay put."

Fly left without saying anything further. I lay there staring at the dark, until the line of light that marked the door suddenly blossomed and the switch clicked the room into a bright, painful glare.

Lisa said, "You're sure a trouble maker, Ryan."

A long time ago Lisa Williams had been a beautiful doll. She had soloed at the Copa, done two musicals on Broadway and seemed headed for Hollywood. She was still beautiful in one way. There weren't many girls who were built like her. She was one full breasted, heavy-thighed bundle of sex that was a marvel to look at. Then you reached her face. Something had happened to it. A car accident could have done it. So could a pair of brutal fists. Big Primo Stipetto didn't like his sex machines playing around in other back yards. In his own with his kid brother Penny, it was even worse.

I said, "Hello, Lisa. It's been pretty long."

"Hasn't it though." She paused, looked quickly at her

hands, then said absently, "What'd you want to get messed up with Big Step for?"

"I didn't know I was."

"He's real old fashioned, Ryan. Anyone who touches his kid brother goes face to face with him. You shouldn't 've killed the kid."

"Look . . . I didn't kill the kid."

"Oh Ryan . . ."

I sucked my breath in, held it and shook my head to clear it. "Penny Stipetto was a cinch to get bumped one day. So he came after me and if he had tried it I would have taken him apart. Somebody else did it, though. Not me."

"Ryan . . . I . . ."

"Forget it, kid."

She watched me a moment, biting her lower lip between her teeth. "I can't forget it. I remember . . . other things."

"Well don't then."

"That's not easy to do."

"Give it a hard try."

"Don't be so damn tough, Irish. Maybe I just don't like to be in somebody's debt. Ever think of it that way? Just because you kept that crazy Doe Wenzel from shooting me and took the slug yourself . . . oh, hell."

"Listen," I told her, "forget the bit. You don't owe me anything."

A cramp caught at the muscles in my lower back and I arched against the ropes. I could feel the tendons pull taut from my neck down and for a full minute the paralyzing agony of the thing held me rigid.

Before I could stop her she was on her knees crying softly, her fingers tearing at the knots on the rope and then suddenly I was free to move and the relief of it was almost too much to take. I lay there and tried to come back to normal slowly and when I made it I said, "Thanks."

"Who was I fooling anyway," Lisa said.

We both heard the door slam out front at the same time. I waved her out quickly, shut the door and put my ear to it. Fly came back in the other room, breathing hard, his voice tight with excitement. "I got Big Step right off on the phone. By damn, he's coming over now. You hear that . . . now. We'll have a real party, by damn. That wise punk'll get his good for sure now. We're gonna do it right here in about five minutes. Boy, I'm gonna enjoy tellin' that punk!"

His feet came across the room, he yanked the door open and there I stood, grinning at him. It took a good three seconds before his hopped up mind realized the full implications of what he was seeing, then before he could move I chopped one across his jaw to shut him down. I put too much mad behind it. He was too small and I was too big for so much mad. He half flew back across the room, skidding on his back, then rolled once and lay in a soft heap with blood running down his chin and his breath dragging in through a twisted jaw.

I found my .45 in his waistband, then probed through his pockets for the capsule. When I didn't find it I tried the seams, the linings, his shoes and every place he could have had it on him. But it wasn't there.

Lisa said suddenly, "Ryan . . . Big Step . . ."

I nodded. "Yeah. Five minutes." I had maybe two left. I couldn't afford to take the chance on staying. I got up, looked at her squarely and said, "He took a cap off me. I need it." When her eyes went funny I added, "I'm not on the stuff. There was something else in that cap besides H."

"I'll . . . I'll try," she said hesitantly.

"Okay baby. And thanks again. Just tell Primo Stipetto Fly did a lousy job tying me up. Now hold still a second."

She saw what I was going to do and never moved. I hit her just right so there could be no doubt about what happened when Big Step came in. I put her down easy and got out of there.

I got word to Pete-the-Dog to meet me at Tony Bay's deli and he left his news stand long enough to fake picking up a sandwich. It was a smart move because Pete told me both Newbolder and Schmidt had been alternating holding a steady stakeout on my apartment and detailed a guy new to plainclothes to watch him and a few others on the block. Homicide had a blanket over the area and I was to be the pigeon.

Pete said, "You're nuts to move around daytimes, Ryan."

"I got no choice, kid. Look you hear any word about Penny Stipetto?"

"Word? Man, that's all I hear. You're their boy, you know that."

"But you know better."

"Sure," Pete nodded, "I do, but I ain't Big Step. After the other brother catching it he's laying it all on you. I'm hearing thing's would scare a snake."

"I got a favor coming, Pete?"

"Anytime. Just anytime."

"Start asking. Somebody around must've seen something when Penny got it."

"In this town two blocks away is somebody else's turf, Irish. Over there they're more scared of the Stipettos than they like you. These days it's real nervous."

"So ask around. Don't stick your neck out, but see what you can pick up."

"Okay, I can do that. Who you want off your neck first, the fuzz or Step?"

I grinned at him, just a little guy, a nobody with a paper stand, but a heart as big as your hat and ready to do anything for a friend he was asked to.

"Any help in either direction will be fine," I told him.

He let out a low chuckle and picked up his wrapped sandwich. "Boy, your connections sure went sour fast. I thought you had an in with the fuzz after that job last year. I thought you was some kind of hero."

"Nobody's nothing with the murder squad when they think you pulled a big hit. They gave me one break. They won't give me two."

"Tough. Anything you want from the house?"

"No. I can get in if I want to. Better if I stayed away though. If you pick up anything, call me at Andy's."

"Right."

I plucked a late copy of the paper from his pocket. "This mine?"

Pete-the-Dog nodded, grinned and walked away. I took the paper out the back door with barely a nod at Tony Bay and opened it up in the alley.

My publicity was a full page wide.

In brief, it stated that in an attempt to apprehend a suspected killer, a gunfight ensued with the wanted man's confederates during which time four persons were killed and several injured. Among the dead were Vincent (Little Step) Stipetto, Carl Hoover and Moe Green, associates of the notorious Primo (Big Step) Stipetto. The other dead man was identified as one Lewis Coyne, address unknown. Two other men engaged in the gunfight escaped, as did "Irish" Ryan, the one suspected of having gunned down Fred (Penny) Stipetto.

For a street shooting of that size, the account was awfully vague. I was suspected of being a target for the Stipettos, yet accused of having them on my side, their diversionary shooting getting me off the hook. Nobody seemed to have pieced the thing together and if they had, it wasn't given to the reporters.

Karen Sinclair was listed as critically wounded and taken to Bellevue Hospital and identified as a secretary in the FCC offices in Manhattan, but that was all.

And I was in the middle of a real fine mess. Like before, everybody wants to kill me and while they try I'm supposed to deliver a lost state secret to somebody who will nab me if I do.

Great life for a hood.

From a luncheonette near Seventh I called the hospital. I gave a phony name, said I was an AP correspondent and queried the operator about the condition of Karen Sinclair. Habit got the better of her and she put me through to the floor. Someone told me Karen Sinclair was still on the critical list and not available for an interview. I thanked them and hung up. I changed phones before making the next call, figuring that if the Sinclair dame had been telling the truth, there'd be Federal fuzz running down every lead they got.

The operator at the precinct house switched me into the office and a heavy voice said, "Newbolder speaking."

"This is Ryan, Sergeant."

After a moment's heavy pause Newbolder said in a bored tone, "All right, boy, where are you?"

"Public phone. Don't bother tracing it. I'll be out of here in a minute."

He knew it and I could tell he wasn't going to be bothered trying. Maybe he was still remembering last year. "Are you coming in?"

"Not yet. I have something I have to do first."

"Oh?" His voice was too soft.

"Let's get something straight first. Don't waste time trying to hang Penny Stipetto's killing on me. I didn't pull it off. I had nothing at all to do with that hit. You poke around for another angle and you'll get some answers."

He didn't answer me at first, then he said quietly, "I didn't think you did. You looked good for it though. Besides, you'd be better off in custody than having Big Step breathing down your throat."

"He doesn't bother me."

"No? Well he bothers me now. He's ready to blow the top off things."

"Let him. What about the Sinclair girl?"

Newbolder came back too fast. "What about her?"

"She talk?"

He still spoke too fast. "What would she have to say?"

"That's what I'm wondering."

"Damn you, Ryan . . ."

"She's in the picture, Sergeant. That mess last night wasn't all me. Big Step had his men out there waiting for me, but she was something right out of the blue."

"Ryan . . ." I knew he was signalling for a tracer now and cursing himself for not having put one on the phone before.

I said, "I'll call you back, kiddo," and hung up.

Now the bit was tighter than ever.

Until now Newbolder had figured that the Sinclair dame sitting with me was a pure accident and I took advantage of the diversion she stirred up outside to take off. Now he was figuring me as being part of a larger picture. In a way it was good. I could always get the fuzz for company real fast if I needed them.

Chapter 3

THE DAY man at the Woolsey-Lever Hotel was Lennie Ames and he owed me a favor. Two years ago he had been making book right at the desk when a team from vice came in to tag him, only I spotted them first, picked up his briefcase of receipts, markers and cash and walked off with the evidence. He got them back after the heat was off and never had the nerve to get in the game again. And I hadn't asked for the favor back until now.

When I walked into the shabby, off-Broadway hotel, Lennie Ames spotted me coming through the door and turned white. Like everybody else, he had seen the papers, only he knew what was coming up. With the barest nod of his head he motioned toward the office and I went in, shut the door and waited. Two minutes later Lennie came in quickly, eased the door closed and plunked down in his chair behind the desk. "Irish . . . for Pete's sake . . ."

Before he could finish I said, "I'm collecting now, buddy."

"Does it have to be me? Man, ever since those hustlers got rousted off Eighth they've been operating out of here. Every night some plainclothes dick comes prowling around. Yesterday there's an investigator from the D.A.'s office in asking questions . . ."

"All I want is a room and no trouble."

"You already got the trouble."

"That's something I have to clean up."

He got up, walked to the window and peered out through the venetian blinds, then closed them all the way. "Look, Ryan, the cops I can steer off, but suppose that Stipetto mob tracks you here? You think they won't put things together? They know what you did one time. So they'll squeeze me and I squeeze easy. I'm chicken, man. I'm ready to run right now. Big Step will put a slug in me as fast as he will you if he knows I'm hiding you out."

"I don't remember waiting to be asked to do a favor that last time, Lennie."

He looked at me, his eyes mirroring his embarrassment. "Okay, Irish, so I was a heel for a while." He grinned at me and tried to light a cigarette with hands that shook enough so that it took two matches to do it. "We keep a spare on the fourth floor northwest corner. It's marked MAINTENANCE SUPPLIES and has an exterior fire escape exit that leads down to the courtyard in back. There's a john, a wash basin and a cot in there and you don't have to register. The handyman who used it died in a sanatarium three months ago and we've been contracting our maintenance work, such as it is. Any questions, you tell them you and he made the arrangements. Leave me out of it."

"Good enough. What about the night manager?"

"A screaming fag afraid of his own shadow. He's had a lot of trouble and we're the only ones who'll give him a job. He'll do anything to keep it. I'll take care of him."

"You'll tell him then?"

"Damn right. It's better they know. I'll tell him you'll land on him like a ton of bricks if he opens his mouth." Lennie pulled the drawer out, threw me a key and said, "It's all yours now. Don't do me any more favors and I won't do you any."

"Sure," I said, pocketed the key and left.

It was only a little cubicle, but it was enough. I could sweat out the days there and use the phone if I had to. The door had a barrel bolt on the inside and the window went up easily. I cased the yard, spotted a handy exit through the six foot fences if I needed it, then flopped down on the cot.

Now was a time for thinking.

I had walked into one hell of a mess. Big Step thought I knocked off his brother and I had the motive, the ability and the time to do it. So he was after me.

The fuzz took the same attitude on recommendation from their varied sources of information and were scouring the city for me. I had a record of arrests even if there were no convictions and they'd love to see me take a fall. I had been in their hair too damn long.

Karen Sinclair was next. If she told me straight, and there was no reason for her not to, I was right in the middle of somebody else's game. She claimed to be a Federal agent and nobody was saying anything. Her job with the FCC could be a great cover. She had passed me something that could make or break our national security and I boffed it.

Damn it, I felt like one hungry trout in a small pond on the opening day of the fishing season! A lousy rabbit that accidentally jumped the fence into a pen of starving hounds.

First move then: I could clean Big Step off my back and the fuzz too if I found Penny Stipetto's killer. But that left Karen Sinclair and the ones she spotted tailing her. That left a whole damn Federal agency who would be breathing down my throat for that capsule.

And Fly had that.

So find Fly first. Go into Big Step's back yard and find Fly. It wasn't going to be easy. The little weasel never holed up in the same place twice and slept in as many doorways as he did beds, but he did leave himself wide open on one count . . . he had told Lisa he was hurting for a blast and thought the cap he took from me was heroin. If it was, there could be trouble. If it wasn't, the trouble was even worse. I had to find out.

Dusk came a little after seven and as soon as the supper crowd had cleared the streets I went back downstairs, got a scared glance from the gay boy at the desk and went outside to the drugstore on the corner and put in a call to Bill Grady who did a syndicated column across the nation and waited for him to answer.

His secretary asked me who I was and I gave the name of the State Senator. It got action fast. She told me he was at his hotel, gave me the number to call and before she could notify him I had my dime in the slot and was dialing.

I said, "Grady?"

"Roger. Who's this?"

"Irish."

There was silence for a second, then: "Boy, you sure don't fool around. Where are you?"

"Not too far away. Can we talk?"

"Come on up."

"There's a statute about aiding and abetting."

"So I've heard. There's also freedom of the press and the unwritten law of protecting news sources. I smell a story."

"Ten minutes."

"I'll be waiting. Alone."

Bill Grady lived in a hotel on West Seventy-Second Street, an old conservative place left over from a different era. I took the elevator up to his floor, touched the buzzer and when he opened the door, stepped inside. I hadn't seen him for three years, but it didn't make any difference. We were still a couple of Army buddies who had a short lifetime together and nothing had changed.

We had one drink before he nodded to a chair and said, "Sit down and talk. You're the hottest item in town."

I shook my head. "It only looks that way, friend."

"Oh?"

"Are we off the record?"

"Natch. Shoot."

So I told him. When I finished he still hadn't touched his drink, but his face looked tight and his fingers were bloodless around the glass in his hand. I said, "What's the matter?"

He took a sip of his highball and put the glass down. "You've just confirmed something that's been a rumor if I read it right."

"So tell me."

Grady hesitated, debating within himself what he should let out. Finally he turned around and stared at me. "I trusted you with my life a few times. I don't see why you'd blow the whistle on this. Have you read about the Soviet oceanography work going on since '46?"

"Some. They've been mapping the ocean floor, studying currents, tidal effects, marine life and all that jazz. Why?"

"You know how the Polaris missile works, don't you?"

"Compressed air fired from a submerged vessel until airborne then rocket effect takes over with a guidance system to the target. Where does that come in?"

"The Reds have been working in International waters about twenty miles off our coasts for years. There's nothing we can do about it except keep them under surveillance. Supposing they developed a Polaris-type missile and located them on a permanent pad a few miles from our shorelines. A half dozen could destroy our major seaport cities, population and military bases with one touch of a button. They could sit there undetected until they were ready to be used and then we'd have it."

"You said they were under surveillance."

"Irish buddy, the ocean is a big place. Submarine development and underwater exploration has come a long way. They could have had decoys going while the real thing sneaked up past our screen and while we're tangled in nuclear disarmament talks and peace treaties, playing big brother to all the slobs in the world, the Soviets are laying the groundwork for our own destruction if the surface negotiations don't go their way. Like idiots, our military appropriations don't allow for full protection. The jerks who handle the loot fight a war in Viet Nam with WWII aircraft, let our guys get killed, they yank out MacArthur who could have won the Korean thing, they make us look stupid around the globe and dig their own graves while they all try to soak up newspaper space so they can run for office when they get promoted up and out."

"Get to the point."

Bill Grady nodded and made himself another drink. He swirled the ice around in the glass and took a swallow from it. "From unauthorized sources, I hear Karen Sinclair was a Fed, all right. I checked her b.g. and she was an Oceanography major at a west coast university. She started out on an assignment with six others, all of whom have died under peculiar circumstances. A further check puts her with a relatively unimportant Navy department engaged in subsurface research, ostensibly charting the shelf off our coast. Let's suppose her job was a secret one, to locate these possible underwater missile sites. Let's suppose she did. You think the Soviets wouldn't be aware of their presence and try to stop it? But let's suppose she alone got away with a record of their positions somehow. They couldn't afford to let her live. She couldn't be left to make her contact. They would have put every resource at their command to nail her and it looks like they might have . . . and you, my friend, were entrusted with the goodies."

I got up, my lips tight across my mouth. "Why me?"

"Because she had to do something and you look like you do."

"Nuts!" I slammed the drink down and glared at him. "That's too damn many suppositions. I don't like any of them."

Quietly, he said, "Suppose they're true?"

"Why the hell do I have to get trapped in the middle?"

"Kismet, my friend. Maybe you're lucky." He took a pull of the drink again. "Or maybe all of us are." Then he looked at me and waited.

"All right, Grady, cut it fine. If I go to the cops they slap my can in a cell for homicide. I sweat. If I tap the Feds they turn me over to the cops anyway. If I give them the story they won't believe me because I can't come up with a lousy capsule and Karen Sinclair isn't able to talk. If she dies, I'll be dead too. If I prowl the streets, either Big Step hits me or the cops do, so where does that leave me?"

For the first time Bill Grady let out a sardonic laugh. "I don't know, old buddy, but it's going to be mighty interesting. Even your obituary written from a speculative viewpoint ought to buy new readers."

"Great. Thanks a bunch."

"No trouble."

"And where do you go from here?"

His grin got bigger. "Nowhere. I'm going to sit back and watch. I want to see a big war hero who digs the hood bit turn patriotic, not because he wants to, but because he has to. It will be an interesting study in human behavior. You've always been an enigma to everybody, now here's your chance to be an even bigger one. All I want is the story."

"Go screw yourself."

"Physically impossible," he laughed again. "It's you who's screwed. To make it worse I went and upset your weird idea of morality and now I want to see the action. You got no choice any longer, Irish. You're the only one who knows all the facts you have to get out of the trap. If you do and when you do, I'll rate a scoop bonus. How about that?"

I put my glass down and stood up. "Maybe, Bill, maybe."

"What's with the maybe?"

"I might need a liaison man. If you want the story, then you're tagged."

He licked his lips, slammed one hand into the other and said, "I might have figured it. So what do you want?"

"Get me in to see Karen Sinclair."

"It can't be done. You'll be spotted. She's got a uniformed police guard and a dozen of the pretty boys stationed around her room. It's impossible."

"So do it anyway," I told him.

At ten p.m. a makeup man from NBC dropped a curly headed rug over my short hair, fitted me with a London mustache, clear-lensed glasses and with a Graflex in my hand, I passed for a Manchester newspaperman whose press card had been lifted from a passed-out owner an hour before. We both had to put down a gallon of ginger ale before he went out on double scotches, but it worked and we made the front desk where a police spokesman told us Karen Sinclair was still too critical to be interviewed. A group of other reporters gave us the laugh for making the try and went back to playing cards on an upside down tray set on their knees.

But Grady didn't stop there. He got the plainclothes man down in the lobby. "Look, maybe she can't talk, but all we want to do is make sure."

The cop said, "Sorry, she isn't to be seen."

"Maybe there's more here than we know about. Since when do innocent bystanders in a shooting get this kind of treatment? I think a little legwork might come up with a tasty bit."

The young guy in the blue gabardine frowned. "Listen . . ."

"I don't listen to anybody. I write, mister. I do a column and have *carte blanche* and if you want it that way, I can raise a lot of interesting questions."

"Wait here a minute," the guy said. He walked to a phone, dialed a number and spoke for a good two minutes. When he came back he nodded for us to follow him. "You can take a look . . . that's all. She's out cold and there's nothing more to it than that. She has a police guard because of this Stipetto business and she might have been a possible eye witness to what happened."

I picked it up quicker than Grady did. "What do you mean . . . what happened?"

The guy was trapped. All he could do was say, "Sorry but . . ."

Before he could turn away I grabbed his arm. "You mean there was more than the shooting?"

When he turned around he was composed again, his face inscrutable. "If you're a police reporter you know what I mean about eye witnesses. Now if you want to see the dame, you have one minute to take a look."

"Sure, but you know us," I said. "Always questions."

"Yeah, but keep it quiet. You'll be the first ones allowed in for a look, and no pictures," he added, pointing to my camera.

I acknowledged and slapped the Graflex shut. The elevator took us to the sixth floor where our guide led us past the others stationed at strategic points along the corridor. The doctor met us at the door, told us to be quick and make no noise, then turned the knob, spoke to the nurse inside and let us pass.

Somebody had taken off Karen Sinclair's makeup and for the first time, I saw her as she was. Even lying there, her face waxen pale, she was a stunning woman, the sheets adhering to every contour of that magnificent body, the lustrous gleam of her chestnut hair framing her beauty. One shoulder was swathed in bandages and another bandage was outlined at her waist.

The nurse beside us reached for her pulse automatically, seemed satisfied and laid her arm back down. "How badly was she shot?" I asked her.

"Luckily, clean wounds. The bullets missed vital organs."

"Is she out of danger?"

"That is for the doctor to say. Now if you don't mind . . ." She walked to the door and held it open. Grady followed her, but I hesitated just a moment. There was a barely perceptible flicker of her eyelids, then they opened slightly and she was looking at me.

I had to do it quickly. I had to make myself known and hope she could think fast despite her condition. I knew I was unrecognizable by my face, but I could duplicate a situation. Without moving my lips, I said softly, "What was the powder in the capsule? Was it heroin?"

For a half second there was no response, then she got it. In the same way, with no motion, her voice a whisper, she said, "Powdered sugar." Then her eyes closed again and I walked away.

Our impatient guide who waited for us in the corridor said, "Satisfied?"

Bill nodded and shrugged. "Sorry to bother you. It's nice to be sure."

"The press will be officially notified of any changes. We'd appreciate it if you would not speculate and stay with the communiques."

"Sure." Bill looked at me. "Let's go. Thanks for the tour."

The guy bobbed his head. "Don't mention it . . . to the other reporters, I mean."

When we were on the steps outside the hospital, I steered Grady to one side and held a match up to the cigarette in his mouth. "They have something hot on this one. Did you get what he said in the beginning?"

"About what happened?"

"Yeah."

"Let's make a phone call. I have a solid in at headquarters. They'll feed me any action if I promise not to let it out until it's cleared."

We crossed the street to a drug store and I waited while Bill put in his call. When he came out of the booth his face was serious, his eyes dark with concern. He sucked nervously on the cigarette and let the smoke stream through his nostrils. "Well?"

"You could have been the key, Irish," he told me. "She was an agent, all right."

"That wasn't what you had on your mind."

He dropped the butt and ground it out under his heel. "The police recovered the spent slugs and matched them with the guns. The shots that hit her didn't come from the police or Stipetto guns. Bullets from those guns got Vincent Stipetto and Moe Green too." He looked at me hard. "Can you break it down now?"

"I think so," I said, "the Stipetto mob was laying for me. When she came out the others starting banging away and the Stipetto boys were caught in between and thought it was part of a crash out on my part. They never lived long enough to find out different. Then Newbolder and Schmidt made the scene and nailed the rest of the gang. In the meantime, the others saw Karen go down and since they thought they nailed their target, they cut out. All the cops saw was the Stipetto boys, tied them in with me and didn't look any further."

"Until now," he mused.

"And where do they go from here?"

"No place until the Sinclair woman can talk. She's the crux. She brought the thing to a head. Trouble is, none of it's over. She's still alive and you're still free."

"And you got my obituary already written."

"No," Bill said, "but I'm thinking of it."

Chapter 4

THROUGH Pete-the-Dog I passed the word down the street to start scratching for Fly. He was hooked on H and someplace he had to locate a source of supply so he'd be hitting a dealer. If he tried mainlining with the sugar in the capsule he'd find out in a hurry he had nothing going for him and would do a crazy dance to get a charge. He wouldn't even try to be careful and the word would go out like a brush fire. What I had to hope for was that he wouldn't discard the microfilm in the capsule where I couldn't find it. A junkie with a big hurt is liable to do anything. If I was lucky he'd keep the cap for a reserve and stick with his regular pusher. He had been in the business long enough to have solid contacts but let trouble touch a hophead and everybody steered clear. Right now little old Fly could have trouble if I knew Big Step. For letting me bust loose he could be getting the hard squeeze.

Chuck Vinson's saloon had a side entrance and I didn't have to go through the bar to snag a booth in the back room. I took the furthest one back and pushed the button for the waiter. Old Happy Jenkins came shuffling back, napkin over one arm and a bowl of pretzels in his hand. He had to peer at me over his glasses a second before he saw who it was, then he swallowed hard and looked back toward the front with eyes suddenly scared.

"You bugs, Irish? You outa your mind? What the hell you doon in here?"

"Trying to get a beer," I said.

"A half hour ago Big Step himself come in asking. Chuck said he ain't seen you but it don't mean they ain't covering from outside."

"So I'm all shook up over it. Do I get that beer?"

"Irish . . . come on. Step had that new guy with him— the one from Miami. They're looking, man. They want you bad."

"Doesn't everybody?"

He licked his lips again and edged in closer. "The cops got a tail on Step in case he finds you. You know that too?"

"It figures. Now get me a tall Piel's with a foamy head

like you see on TV and I'll blow. And ask Chuck if I got any phone calls."

Happy nodded joylessly and shuffled off. Two minutes later he was back with a Stein, slid it over in front of me and said, "You got a call from somebody." He handed me a matchbook cover with a number scrawled on it. "You gotta buzz 'em back. Chuck says not to use his place like an office while the heat's on."

When he left I finished half the beer, found a dime and hopped into the phone booth beside me. The number was a Trafalgar exchange which put it somewhere in the West Seventies but I didn't recognize it. The phone rang just once before it was picked up and a cautious voice said, "Yeah?"

"Irish. You call?"

"Where you at?"

"Chuck Vinson's."

That seemed to satisfy him. He said, "Pete-the-Dog saw me today. Said you wanted to know about Fly."

"Got anything?"

"No, but I know where he gets his junk from. He was peddling for Ernie. Ernie paid him off in H. If you want Fly, try him."

"Thanks buddy. What do I owe you?"

"Nothin'. You took me out of a jam once. We're square now" He hung up abruptly and I stood there for a minute trying to figure out who it was. Hell, a lot of people owed me favors. I went back, finished my beer and went out the same way I came in, mixing with a group going past the door to the subway station.

Ernie South had started off in the wholesale candy business fifteen years ago, working the fringe areas of Harlem before he switched to dope. He had peddled the stuff for Treetop Coulter before he took his first fall, did his time in Sing Sing, then came back and muscled Treetop right out of the business. He wound up operating in Big Primo Stipetto's territory, managed to get himself in the good graces of the boss and ran a neat operation the cops weren't able to break.

Everybody had been hearing a lot about Ernie South lately. He and Penny Stipetto were thick as blood brothers, especially since '62 when Big Step turned over a prime section uptown to his kid brother to run as he saw fit. Penny Stipetto had been on the verge of being a big time operator when he was knocked off and since they thought I was his killer, Ernie South would have his hands out looking for me too. Penny's death left the section wide open and until Big Step moved back in or designated another lieutenant to handle it, Ernie was moving things around.

Damn it! I should have kept my hands to myself, but when Penny tore into old Rudy Max and broke him up for not paying protection money to operate a news stand I couldn't help myself. I broke his jaw and four ribs and left him in a mess of his own blood on the side walk, not giving a damn how big he or his brothers were. Two of his men were right there when it happened and neither of them had the guts to go for a rod because they knew I had a blaster in my belt and would chop them down the second they moved. They had seen it happen before. No, they could wait. Big brother Step would take care of it if Penny didn't. Only Penny Stipetto didn't want to look like a lily with everybody waiting to see how he took it. No, he had to go gunning for me himself.

And somebody else nailed him.

Why?

It didn't take too much doing to locate Ernie South. I had enough friends in the area who didn't dig the narcotics bit and had seen too much heat brought in on their own operations because of his. They were glad to pinpoint him at a sleezy gin mill that featured a belly dancer, and let me work out my own arrangements with him. They knew damn well there was a price on my head from all directions, but they had lived under the shake-down racket Big Step ran too long to help him out any. All I got was a word to watch myself, a couple offers of an assist I waved off and a silent word that meant they hoped I could make something stick.

For an hour and a half I stood across the street waiting, watching the customers come and go until the place was almost empty. Then, through the window, I saw Ernie flip a bill to the bartender, say something they both thought was funny, then go to the door.

He was looking west watching for a cab when I put the nose of the .45 in his ribs and said, "Hello, Ernie."

Even before he turned around he started to shake like he was going to come apart at the seams. He stiffened, seemed to rise on his toes and twisted just enough to see me. Then his eyes met mine briefly and a smile flickered across his mouth and he relaxed until he was almost casual. "You're taking big chances these days, Irish."

"Not from you, punk." I nudged him with the gun, ran

my hand over his pockets and beltline to make sure he wasn't heeled and said, "Start walking. Get out of line just once and you've had it, boy." I wasn't putting on an act. I'd scatter his guts over the street as fast as I'd look at him and he knew it, but he knew it didn't have to happen either so he simply shrugged and turned toward Broadway and strolled along with me at his side like a couple of buddies.

"You're in the wrong end of town, Irish. Big Step has his people all over the place."

"Then hope we don't meet any. You'll catch the first one."

I saw his nervous glance to both sides of the street, hoping nobody would show. Hopheads Ernie could handle. Me he couldn't. "What's the gimmick?" he asked.

"We never tangled. I'm not any part of the show."

"I want Fly. He peddled around for you and you supplied his H. Where is he?"

"How the hell should I know?"

"The last time I saw him he needed to blast bad. You're his source."

Ernie South didn't answer me. He reached for a cigarette and lit it with a hand that shook badly.

I said, "Ernie, I'm going to point this rod at your leg. I'm going to put one right through the back of your knee and roll out of here before a squad car can get near the place. You'll be going around on an aluminum and plastic peg the rest of your life."

He tried to sound calm about it. "You wouldn't do it."

"Remember Junior Swan? Ever see his hands? He can't use either of them now. Remember Buck Harris and Sy Green? Sy's mind is going on him now and Buck is still in a wheelchair in a charity ward trying to forget that night."

Ernie remembered all right. I could see the sweat on his forehead glistening under his hatbrim. He swallowed, wiped his hand across his face and half whispered, "So Fly's on the *out* list. He don't get a thing from nobody."

"Why?"

"Because Big Step said so. He's making Fly hurt for doing a dumb thing like he did with you."

"Where is he, Ernie?"

"I don't know! I . . ."

He heard the .45 go off half cock and the tiny click was like a sonic boom in his ears. "Come on, Irish, I don't know where he is. Try somebody else!"

"Name them."

"Cortez maybe. Connie Morse or Joey Gomp on Ninety-Sixth Street. He used to hit them sometimes."

"That's still Big Step's territory."

"Sure, and they're all cuttin' him off. So try downtown. He had some contacts there only don't ask who. My turf is here. I don't know them guys."

I knew he was telling the truth. Ernie South wasn't about to lie to me right then or he knew what would happen. "Where's his pad, Ernie?"

"Basement joint two places down from Steve's Diner on Second."

I caught the expression that came into his face and let him feel a touch of the gun again. "Finish it, Ernie."

He was caught and knew it. If he didn't lay it on the line he knew I'd come looking for him. He said, "Big Step's got a man covering the place."

"Why?"

"So Fly can't make his pad if he's got anything stashed away in there."

"Nice. Step holds a big mad, doesn't he?"

"You'll find out," he said viciously.

"Who killed Penny Stipetto, Ernie?"

He stopped then, turned his head to look directly at me and his eyes were black with hate. His whole face seemed drawn in a tight mask. I grinned at him deliberately and shook my head. "Not me, boy."

"You're dead, Ryan. You might just as well jump in front of a subway and get it over with."

I thumbed the .45 back on half cock again and shoved it under my belt. "When I go it'll be the hard way and it won't be alone. Go tell Big Step I'm looking for him."

He almost ran getting to the corner and when he was out of sight I cut across the street, through an alley and came out the other side, flagged down a cab and told him to take me to the Cafeteria. Big Step, Newbolder, Schmidt and the rest might be looking for me but they wouldn't be expecting me to turn up in a place I ate in five nights a week. Enough of the Broadway crowd would be on hand as usual to pass me any information if they weren't too scared of the action.

Wally Pee was the first one to spot me and he almost spilled his coffee. He gave me the signal that he was no good for talking and let his eyes sidle to the back corner where Izzy Goldwitz was finishing a pot pie with his usual relish. I walked up, got a cup of coffee and took it back to Izzy's table where I sat down with my back to the rest. It could be a fatal mistake, but I didn't want anybody picking me up by sight. Izzy got that sick look again and couldn't finish his pot pie, reaching for his coffee to quiet down what was happening to his stomach.

When he put the cup down his eyes pleaded with me. "Get lost, Irish. Get away from me, huh? You got this town on its ear already and I don't want to be there when the shooting starts again."

"No sweat, Izzy. All I want is Fly. You see him around?"

"Me, I don't see nothing. Now scram, okay?"

"Fly's hitting all the suppliers."

"I know. Big Step's got him cut off. Fly's taking a cure whether he likes it or not and it'll kill him for letting you off the hook. So whatta you want him for? Another guy was looking for him before. Got Pedro the bus boy all shook?"

I frowned at him. "Who?"

"I dunno. Ask Pedro. Just get away from me."

"Sure, Izzy. Thanks."

"From you I want nothin', not even thanks."

Pedro was a little Puerto Rican with a multiplicity of last names nobody could pronounce who worked his heart out hustling dirty dishes to support six brothers and sisters. He was quick as a banty rooster and always ready with a big smile, but when I found him in the back room off the kitchen he was neither quick nor smiling. He was sitting on an upturned lard bucket, his head in his hands and when I came in he jumped, his face contorted, his hands clutching his belly.

I said, "Hi, Pete."

When he recognized me he tied on a smile but it didn't fit very well and he dropped it. "Mr. Ryan," he acknowledged softly.

"What happened, kid?"

"I theenk nothing happened, please."

With my toe I hooked an empty coke box and set it up so I could squat down beside him. "Let's have it Pete. Who took you apart?"

"It ees nothing."

"Don't kid me. I'll find out anyway, so save yourself some grief. Whoever did it can come back."

Sudden terror filled his eyes and he huddled up against the wall, his teeth biting into his lip. He looked at me, shrugged resignedly. "A man, he look for Fly. He look for you too."

"Who came first?"

"You, Mr. Ryan. He ask about you the other night. I theenk he is police and I tell heem how you left here. I tell heem how Fly was back there waiting too."

"What else?"

"Nothing. I can't tell heem where you are. I tell heem where Fly lives after he hit me."

"Describe him."

"Not beeg as you, Mr. Ryan. Funny voice like I have to speak English, only different. Very bad man. Mad."

"So you know where Fly is?"

He shook his head. "No. I do not see him seence then."

"He was your friend, Pete. You know he was hooked on H?"

"Sure, I know."

"Do you know where he gets his stuff?"

"Before, from Ernie South mostly. Now, I do not know."

"Anybody around here?"

"Nobody will sell to Fly now. He ees in a very bad way, I theenk."

I stood up and rubbed the top of his head. "Okay, kid, thanks. Don't you worry about the guy coming back. Until it's over you'll get a little cover."

"Please, you don't have to . . ."

"No sweat, Pete. No trouble at all." I grinned at him and this time he managed a small smile for real. I said, "There a phone around here?"

He pointed toward the door. "Right inside the kitchen."

I reached Newbolder at his home after the precinct gave me his number. He said, "Sergeant Newbolder speaking, who is this?"

"Your buddy, Irish."

He didn't say anything for a few seconds and I could hear him breathing, then flick on a cigarette lighter. "Okay, I can't put a tracer on your call from here, Irish. Now what's the pitch?"

"There's a kid at the Cafeteria, a bus boy named Pedro. Maybe you'd better keep him covered for a few days. He just took a shellacking from an unknown person that might fit into your case."

I could hear a pencil scratching, then: "You got friends of your own who could do that, Ryan."

"Yeah, I know, but that's what you're for."

"Don't get snotty," he said. "You're after something."

"A hophead named Fly."

"What about him?"

"Has he been seen around?"

"No squawks on him."

"Then you'd better run him down quick before you have a corpse on your hands. Big Step cut off his supply and if he doesn't fold he'll knock off somebody to get a charge."

"Where does he fit in?"

"I'd like to tell you, copper, but if I want out of this mess I have to get out myself."

"You're not doing too well. If you make another day on the streets your luck is running first class."

"I'll play along with it."

"When you get smart, pass it up. Right now that Federal agency you shilled for a couple years ago is breathing down your neck. You're on everybody's 'S' list and it's only a matter of time. Until Big Step moves we can't lay a hand on him and by then it'll be too late, you'll be dead, so I recommend protective custody."

"And a murder charge for bumping Penny Step? No dice, Sarge."

Casually, he said, "Have it your way, friend."

"I will." Then I added, "By the way, how is Karen Sinclair?"

And just as off handedly he said, "I couldn't tell you. An hour ago she was kidnapped from her room."

It was like I had been sapped again. "What?"

"Blame yourself a little, Irish. Try this one on your conscience if you have any."

My fingers squeezed the phone so hard my knuckles turned white. "How was it worked?"

"Two doctors under a gun. The third guy posed as an intern. He shot the guy he took the uniform from in front of the doctors and they had no choice except to go along. They moved her into an ambulance under the guard's noses and got her out. We found the ambulance ten minutes ago, but she could be anywhere by now."

"Damn!"

"So chalk one dead girl up on your list, hood. I think you got the picture pretty well by now. We took Bill Grady in and he had to lay it out for us. You've made everybody a lot of trouble and when you dream, think of that lovely broad stretched out on a slab somewhere."

Under my breath I began swearing, then stopped when I was so tight I wanted to tear the damn phone right off the wall. "They won't kill her," I said.

"No? Why?"

"Because I have what they want and it won't do them a bit of good to bump her unless they know where she dropped the little goodie they're all after."

I hung up then, stared at the phone a minute, then crossed the kitchen and took the back way out through the service entrance. Fly was the key. Someplace he was roaming around carrying a bombshell of information big enough to tear apart the world. *They* knew it and I knew it, but I couldn't get to it without making myself a target for the cops, Big Step and a team of Soviet killers.

The hell I couldn't.

I was looking for a cab when the black Chevy came idling by. The light on the corner was green and in New York you don't loaf when you have the signal on your side. It was too out of character for a cab with N.Y. plates and I had played too many games the same way not to notice it.

Even before the first shot flamed from the window I was down and rolling, scrambling sideways for the cover of the trash cans at the curb and right behind me two more rocketed off the sidewalk with a brief, shrill ricochetting scream before they plastered against the wall. I had just a single look at the face turned my way that was framed in the light of the street lamp, a sharp, hawk-like face under a shock of pitch black hair with one unruly twist of it hanging down into his eyes.

The car was gone around the corner before I could get the gun out and except for a drunk who looked at me soddenly, nobody caught the action. They heard the noise though, even if most of it was contained inside the Chevy. Two couples were dodging traffic to get across the street, but before they made it or I had to offer any explanations, I got up, dusted myself off and started away.

The drunk wiped the drool from his mouth and laughed. "Nice friends you got, mister."

"Only the best," I told him.

So now I was being stalked. Somebody figured I might come back looking for Fly, or word would get to me about somebody looking for him. I was being set up very nicely by a pack of pros and the perimeter of the jungle was getting smaller and smaller. Well, I lived here too and I wasn't going to make it easier for them.

But I wasn't really thinking of myself. I was thinking of the loveliness of Karen Sinclair, the broad who was willing to give her life for a purpose. Now *they* had her . . . and I knew why. To break her out meant a trade . . . the microfilm for her, and even then it was a rotten deal because once they had their information back, she would go under a gun too. And what they wanted was in the possession of a crazy junkie who wouldn't know the time of day when I found him. *If* I found him.

Chapter 5

A COUPLE of years ago a Fed team had me picked up. It wasn't a pinch, though I would have been better off if it were. It was a cute pressure play because they wanted my peculiar services at their command since it was the only way they could handle a project. They laid my neck on the line and I had no choice about it so I played cop with them and came out of the deal a hood-type patriot and it took a long time to wash the smell of the association out of my system. My kind of people didn't go along with any kind of cops, even a recruited hood.

Now the time for returning favors was back again. The card in my wallet was worn at the edges and a few odds and ends were scribbled across the face, but the number was still legibile and I called it. Somebody was always at that office night and day and I wasn't worried about getting an answer at this hour. The phone was lifted and a voice said, "Varlie Imports, what can I do for you?"

"Try remembering me for a starter," I said.

"Yes?" The voice was puzzled.

"The name is Ryan . . . the Irish one as you used to call me."

"One moment, please." Sound diminished as he held a hand over mouthpiece and I could barely hear the hum of voices. Then the hand was taken away and the voice that spoke to me was a different one, but one I remembered well.

There was nothing friendly there. It was cold and impersonal and said, "What do you want, Ryan?"

"To see you, Shaffer. You're picking up a tab for *me*."

"Ryan . . ."

"Uh-uh. I'll do the talking. I'm in a pay station and you can't trace the call in time so don't bother. Just go to the corner of Eighth Avenue and Forty-Fifth Street and start walking north on the west side. When I'm sure you're alone I'll contact you. Twenty minutes, that's all you have." I hung up and grinned to myself. Cliff Shaffer would be there, all right. He knew what the picture was well enough.

I knew he'd make a try for a pinch anyway so I had a

114

friend of mine who had an independent cab out in front of the car he had stationed near the corner and block its way. Before Shaffer went fifty feet I was behind him, steered him into the hotel lobby on the corner and angled to the east-west street and started him walking. I didn't have to use the gun. Shaffer never did trust me all the way and wasn't taking any chances. When he knew I had caught the play in time, he shrugged it off and played the game. He hadn't bothered wearing a rod either.

Two blocks over was an all night diner and we had coffee and sandwiches sent back to our table and I looked at him sitting there, still the same, case hardened cop he had always been, a little grayer now with a few more wrinkles at the corners of his eyes, but a guy who headed up a tight little agency assigned to special high-priority projects only.

He looked at me just as carefully and said, "You haven't changed much, Irish."

"I'm still alive."

"For how long? There's a city wide alert on you. Or maybe Big Step will reach you first."

"You left out some tourist types, old buddy."

The hand bringing the match to his cigarette stopped in midair. "You know too much, Ryan."

"No . . . not quite enough. I want to stay alive and you, friend, are going to help out."

"Like hell. What you did before doesn't carry any weight now. You're just another hood to me and if I can nail you for the city boys it'll be my pleasure." He glared at me and finished lighting his butt.

"Let's put Karen Sinclair in this," I said. "Let's not make me out an idiot. I didn't get asked in, I was forced in by one of your people again and I'm tired of being a pawn."

Softly, he said, "Where do you get your information from, Irish?"

"I was a college boy once, remember? I was a war hero. I'm clever."

"You're a damned hood."

"So I like it this way. I can chisel the chiselers and don't have to pay any respect to the phony politicos who run us into the ground for their own egotistical satisfaction. I don't have to go along with the sheep who cry and bleat about the way things are and can do something about it in my own way. If this was 1776 I'd be a revolutionary and tax collectors would be fair game. I could drop the enemies trying to destroy us and be a wheel. So screw it, I'm not going to be a sheep."

His icy gray eyes ran over my face and his smile was almost deadly. "Let's talk about Karen Sinclair."

"And oceanography?" I needled him. "Or would a strip of microfilm be better, one that locates all the underwater missile pads the Soviets laid off our coastline?"

With feigned calmness Shaffer folded his hands together and leaned forward on the table. "I didn't think it was possible. I didn't think coincidence could be so damn acute. We all wondered and tried to put it together and nothing would fit."

"The ones who tailed her put it together fast enough."

He ignored me completely, following his own train of thought. "So you're the one she passed it on to. She was able to say that much but couldn't make a positive identification. We knew but we weren't sure. We didn't think it could have happened like that."

"Who are they, Shaffer?"

"Where is it, Irish?"

"Who are they?" I repeated.

Shaffer let his smile stretch across his mouth, tight and nasty. "Manos Dekker. He's the head of the thing we labeled the *Freddie Project* in Argentina, the one who killed Carlos Amega in Madrid and behind the sabotage in our installations in Viet Nam."

"Now he's here," I stated.

"I'm going to tell you a story, Irish."

"Go ahead."

"They spotted our people supposedly engaged in simple coastwise oceanography. They used a limpet and blew the *Fairway II* apart, but they didn't get the motor launch in time. Karen Sinclair and Tim Reese got away with the charts they had made and Tim microfilmed them in Miami. They got him there too, but by then Karen had the film strips but couldn't deliver because they were right behind her. Somehow she made New York. It didn't do her much good because they have their agents all over and covered all routes and were waiting for her to show up. Luckily, she spotted them and took the big chance. Unluckily, it had to be you. Now where is it?"

"Get me off the hook and maybe you'll find out."

Gently, he unlaced his fingers and shook out another cigarette. "What?"

"I know where it is. I might be able to recover it. I

can't do it with the cops on my neck. I can't fight a murder charge and the Stipettos at the same time."

"Sorry, Irish."

"In that case, so am I. You'll lose an agent and all she worked for."

"Damn it, Irish . . ."

"Just do it," I said, "I don't care how. You guys have the power so make things move. You did it once before when I didn't want it, so do it now when I do or I'll resurrect that deal all over again and blow it wide open in the papers."

"Patriotism, Irish."

"Don't bother naming it. I'm saving my own neck."

"How about Karen Sinclair's? You seem to have a soft tone when you say her name."

Soft? I couldn't get her out of my mind. Ever since I saw her that's all I could think about.

"Knock it off, Shaffer. Are you coming through?"

"This time I don't have the choice, do I?"

"No."

"I'm wondering about something else too," he said. "You'd like to process this so you come out clean, wouldn't you?"

I watched him and waited.

Shaffer smiled at me and I couldn't read his face at all. "I'm going to run your gun permit through for you. You're being reactivated, Ryan."

"The hell I am!"

"Then you didn't read the fine print in those papers you signed a couple years ago. The provision was there. The penalties too."

"You bastard. I'm not playing cop again."

"Like you say, Irish boy, 'The hell you ain't.' You know where to reach me. Call in. I'll get some of the heat off your back. You take care of the rest." He got up slowly, his mouth twisting in a wry smile. "Maybe it was a good thing she did pick you out of eight million people. You're just smart enough, mean enough and evil enough to do what has to be done."

"Listen, Shaffer . . ."

But he wouldn't. He shook his head, holding up his hand to cut me off. "We'll have our men out too. We'll scour the city for Karen Sinclair, but we know what we're up against. This isn't a ransom snatch. It was cleverly planned and executed. The ones behind it have a motivation greater than ransom with more resources at their command than the criminal element. But in their own peculiar ways they are criminals and like the old saying goes, it takes one to catch one. Good hunting, Irish. If we can supply any leads just call. You have the number. I suggest you come down and look at our mug shots."

He turned and walked out and I cursed him silently every inch of the way to the door. The slob hung me again with my own kind and there was no turning back. Even getting the heat off wasn't worth it. I liked what I was and wanted to keep it that way and now I was back on the other end of the stick again.

Damn.

Shaffer had clued his office staff. They were all the clean cut type and two of them watched me go over the mug books with narrowed eyes of disapproval. On one's desk was my dossier so I knew they had all the data from the last deal. The broad at the reception desk was the only one who seemed impressed because she took a pose with her legs so I could see the flash of white thigh above her nylons under the desk and when she brought another set of photos over she bent down deliberately to give me the benefit of an unrestricted view of ample breasts that wanted to spill out of her dress. One of the guys tightened his mouth impatiently and threw three eight by ten glossies in front of my nose and waved her out of there. "Manos Dekker," he said.

They weren't studio shots. They were taken with a long range lens and blown up, but the face and all its characteristics were there. Dekker had no stamp of nationality on him, but the set to his eyes, the flaccid mouth and the slight hump in his nose marked him a killer and a man who enjoyed his work. I had seen too many with those almost imperceptible peculiarities not to recognize the breed.

I fastened him in my mind and went back to the selected photos of other agents operating in this country. Two I knew right off, but so did everybody else. In one hazy shot that was evidently an enlargement of individuals originally in a group shot, I thought I had seen another before but couldn't quite place him. The guy at my shoulder caught my hesitation and said, "Taken at a Commie meeting on the Island. Not identified."

I nodded, looked through the book and closed it. "Thanks for the trouble."

"No trouble at all," I told him.

"Any contact with those persons will be reported."

"Sure. Dead or alive?"

"Don't be funny."

Lisa Williams left very little trail. She was always on call for anything Big Step needed and if he wanted to farm her out to his boys for kicks she had to go along. Ever since he destroyed her with his fists she had lived a life of fear, indelibly tied to the punk because his mark was on her and nobody else would touch her. She hustled the upper Broadway johns for side money and spent it in the gin mills, a sucker for a touch from every stray cat type with a hard luck story.

Getting to her without making contacts with any of the Stipetto mob or their stringers who would be happy to pass on the news I was in the territory wasn't easy, but like I said before, it was my city too and there weren't many back alleys or dodges I didn't know. I had to live by them the same way they did only on a bigger scale and it took a hell of a lot more doing.

I found her in the back room of a shabby brownstone at four in the morning, a lonely voice fogged out of shape by too much booze, caroling a song from a stage hit she had been in years ago. When I knocked on the door it was as if someone had lifted the arm on a record player. The quiet was almost intense, and I knew that inside she was standing there rigid, listening hard, her heart pounding with that old fear again.

At last she said, "Yes . . . yes, who is it?"

"Irish, honey, open up."

Very slowly, the door opened on a chain and she peered out at me, eyes reddened from a big bar night, her hair dishevelled, an untidy lock of it falling across her face. "Ryan?" she said tentatively. And when she made sure it was me she bit into a knuckle and shook her head mutely.

"Let me in, girl."

"No . . . please. If anybody sees you . . ."

"Nobody saw me but they might if I stand here long enough." That decided her. She closed the door, took off the chain and held it open reluctantly. I squeezed inside, shut and locked it, then walked across the room and sat on the arm of the mohair chair by the shaded window.

"Why . . . did you come here?"

"I'm looking for Fly. You know where he is?"

She opened her mouth to lie then knew I caught it and

let her head fall into her hands. "Why doesn't Big Step let him alone?" she sobbed jerkily.

"What did he do to you, baby?"

Lisa let her hands fall and hang straight at her sides. "All he could do was hit me. I . . . I didn't care. It was that new one from Miami they call Pigeon who did things." The tears welled up and an expression of shame clouded her face. Without looking at me she sank into a straightback chair and stared at the floor. "That one isn't normal. He . . . he's perverted. He made me . . ."

"You don't have to tell me about it."

"I never did anything like that before, even when they tried to . . . hold me down. He took this . . ."

"Can it, Lisa."

She looked up, her eyes gone dull. "They hurt me. Step laughed and laughed. He thinks I let you go . . . because of those times years ago." Like a slow motion picture she moved her hand and ran her fingers through her hair. A smiled played at the corners of her mouth and she said, "I'm going to kill him some day. Some day. Yes, it will be very nice." There was a sing-song lilt in her voice and only then did I realize how really crocked she was. Constant practice with the bottle and an uncommonly strong constitution provided her with the ability to maintain a semblance of sobriety even when she was almost ready to go off the deep end. Her fear had covered it in the beginning, but now it showed through.

I said, "Where's Fly, Lisa," as gently as I could.

Little by little her eyes came back to mine. "Fly is nice. He always told me when . . . Step wanted me . . . and I would go away. When I was sick . . . he sent a doctor. Yes, yes. He stayed with me a week then."

"And how did you pay him off, Lisa?"

Her smile was unconcerned. "It . . . didn't matter."

"Fly's no better than the rest, kid. Where is he?"

"Are you . . . going to hurt him?"

"No." I leaned forward to center her attention. "He took something from me. I want it back."

She frowned, trying to think, then grimaced and said, "You . . . you hooked, Irish? You can get the . . . junk anytime."

"I'm not hooked, kid. I want that capsule Fly took. Where did he put it?"

"He needs it." There was a defiance in her face I knew I couldn't break.

So I said, "It's only sugar, Lisa. He won't get anything from it but trouble."

It wasn't Fly she cared for. It was the little guy, the creature, the beat-down thing that made him so much like she was herself. It was the two-of-a-kind feeling, people in the same foxhole, wounded and hurting with terrifying death at any moment.

"Is . . . it true?"

I nodded.

Without seeming to cry, the tears began an erratic course down her cheeks. "He put it . . . somewhere. For later, he said. Now he can't go to his place . . ."

"I know, Big Step has one of his boys outside waiting to cut him off."

Absently, she wiped the tears away. "He knows where Ernie South . . . keeps his supply. He was going . . . to break in and . . ." Abruptly, the tears stopped. "You know Ernie South?" she asked me. Some of the drunkenness seemed to have drained out of her.

"We met. He's a bum."

Her mouth tightened. "Irish . . ." she opened her mouth to say something, stopped, reconsidering, then said vacantly, "He's . . . his king . . . heroin . . . the worst of them all."

"Did Fly tell you where he was going?"

"Tarbush's Coffee Shop. Fly . . . he stole Ernie's key once. He had another made."

"He's nuts! Ernie'll chew him up. He can't pull a stunt like that!"

She grinned again and nearly slid off the chair. Her eyes were half closed when she said, "No?" then her head fell forward and I caught her before she hit the floor. Lisa Williams was out like a light but there was still that satisfied grin on her mouth. I picked her up, dropped her in the bed and went out, making sure the door locked shut behind me.

I had just reached the front door of the vestibule when I saw the outline of a figure on the other side. I flattened against the wall, deep in the shadows, glad the overhead bulb was out. The door swung open and the guy standing there smirked to himself. Briefly, I caught the wink of light from the open blade in his hand, then he closed the door silently and started back toward Lisa's room.

When I laid the barrel of the .45 across the back of his head he went down like a withering flower and I grabbed him before he hit the floor. Even in the semi-darkness I could see he was a pasty faced snake with all the evil inside him written across his features. The dark gray suit he wore was the kind they only sell south of Jacksonville and when I yanked the wallet out of his pocket I confirmed it. The driver's license was issued to one Walter Weir of Miami, Florida. I said, "Hello, Pigeon," and slipped the wallet back.

The car he had used was a beat up black Buick ten years old, still carrying Florida tags. Nobody saw me lug him out and if they did, nobody cared. Shouldered drunks weren't unusual around that neighborhood even in the pre-dawn hours. Pigeon Weir did me a favor in a way. It saved hunting up a cab. I drove six blocks North and three across town to where Tarbush ran his coffee shop, an unlikely little place popularized by the trucking crowd rather than the beats. Tarbush had been nailed twice for pushing Bennies on the teenage set and did a stretch in Elmira, but if he was letting Ernie South use his place for a storehouse it looked like he never cut loose from his old connections.

Pigeon wasn't about to come to for a long while yet so I just let him slump there half on the floor out of sight. When I saw the silhouette of a roving prowl car heading toward me, I went down beside him and waited until it passed. Then I slid out of the car and edged toward the narrow alley that separated Tarbush's Coffee Shop from the garage next door.

A night light was on inside, a single low wattage bulb throwing enough of a glow to make out the array of tables and the short counter with its oversized coffee urns. But it wasn't the front section I was interested in. All the side windows were barred, and at the far end was the service entrance, a steel plated door that looked impossible to force. I swore under my breath and out of habit thumbed the latch to check it.

Without a sound, the door swung open inward. The .45 jumped into my hand and I was in with the door closed at my back and the darkness around me like a blanket. If anybody was there with his eyes already tuned to the dark, I could be a perfect target and if I moved, they could pick me out by sound as well. So I stood there waiting, the rod out and showing big and if they saw that, they knew one flash of gunfire would get a barrage back and it might not be worth the chance.

A full minute passed before I knew I was alone. I let my breath out slowly, listening to the stillness, then flicked on a match. I was alone, all right, but only in a way. Crumpled on the floor among the wreckage of cardboard cartons and scattered cans that had spilled out mounds of coffee was the pathetic body of Fly who lay there with his eyes wide open, his neck cocked at a screwy angle and a dark bluish welt on the side of his neck.

Somebody had cooled Fly the hard way. He had torn his clothes apart, ripped open seams and turned the pockets inside out and I knew damn well what he was looking for. But he never found it. Every last possibility had been exhausted and the marks of frustration were there marked by where the body had been kicked a half dozen times.

It wasn't Fly who had opened the cans. If he had, he would have found what he came for. Idly tossed aside were two plastic wrapped packets and it didn't take twenty questions to figure out what they held. Somebody had finished Fly's search for him, not knowing just what it was he was after.

I looked at the body again and saw the bruise under one eye and the smashed lips. The fingernails of one hand were streaked with blood and I knew why he died too. Manos Kekker had picked up Fly's trail somewhere but didn't know he was dealing with a hophead half-crazy from narcotic starvation and Fly put up a fight. It was his last. He was chopped down quickly and efficiently without knowing what it was all about.

The stuff that had been in his pockets was piled on the floor, in the middle of the odds and ends, a new brass key. The match burned out and I lit another, picked up the key and went to the door and fitted it in the lock from the outside. It was the type you had to lock by key when you left with an oversize barrel bolt on the inside. In his haste, Fly hadn't barred the door and left himself wide open for murder.

And the chase was still on.

I locked the door, went out to the car and drove it to the nearest subway station. I pulled in next to a hydrant deliberately, took the knife Pigeon was going to use on Lisa, wrapped a handkerchief around it, and rammed it up to the hilt in his tail. He never even moaned, but he would tomorrow, and he'd get the message loud and clear. I wiped the wheel clean, got out and went down the Kiosk to catch the downtown local.

Chapter 6

STATISTICS say most of all police cases are solved through the use of informants. There are three kinds: stoolies who squeal to ingratiate themselves with the cops, those who talk when the cops put the heat on them one way or another, and those who dump information into HQ anonymously to get the competition out of the way.

But there are others of the night people who know the same things, untouchable in their own way, living by the strange code that separates those of the badge from their own kind. And I was one of them. Once. Until they found out different I'd still be one.

I got to the hotel as the day shift was coming in and I had a chance to get a quick glance at the desk. The night man was just coming on with wrists fluttering all over the place and he looked like a whipped child every time he looked at Ames. The lobby was empty and I crossed to the elevator and as I did Ames spotted me, came around the desk and took me to one side. "You have anything in your room?"

"Nothing worth while. Why?"

"Paul . . . one of the bellboys . . . spotted the fag going in there and let me know about it. I gave him a clout in the mouth. Either he was curious or he was after your skin."

I felt my shoulders start to crawl. "Listen . . ."

"It's okay. He tried that before on somebody who was holing up here because the fuzz was looking for him. Thought he could pressure him into playing his little love games."

"I'll give him pressure."

"Never mind, I took care of it. Just check your stuff. I don't trust any of those AC-DC guys."

"Sure." I slapped his shoulder, threw a dirty look toward the desk and watched the guy turn away with a nervous little squeal. Nothing was missing from the room, but I had run enough shakedowns to know my stuff had been thoroughly searched. Later I'd take care of the guy my own way and he wouldn't go snooping anywhere again.

I called the desk, got Ames just before he left and gave him Pete-the-Dog's number. He was in a state of half sleep it took a couple of minutes to lose but he straightened up the second I told him what I wanted. I gave him the poop on Karen Sinclair's kidnapping from the hospital and told him to spread the news to our people fast. There were always eyes around that saw everything and no matter how good you were, New York had just too many people who never seemed to sleep, whose eyes caught everything and could put the pieces together. Some of those people were ours. Pete said he'd get on it and I flopped back on the bed and closed my eyes.

It was raining when I woke. My watch said ten after five and outside in the premature dusk of fog and rain the offices were beginning to empty, spilling their occupants into taxis and subways. I cleaned up, shaved and got dressed, then headed for the Grand Canyon of New York.

On the corner I picked up a paper, scanning it to see if Fly's body had been found. I was willing to bet it hadn't shown up yet and if the absence of news was an indication, I was right. I scrounged up a box, packed the heroin into it, wrapped it in birthday paper and addressed it to Newbolder at the precinct house. It wouldn't take them long to analyze the grains of coffee still sticking to the packets and locate their source. A few heads would roll and it was doing it the easy way.

Pete-the-Dog ran a news stand that was a clearing house for anything we wanted. He always knew who was under the heat and where the rabbits were holing up and if somebody had to jump fast to stay ahead of the fuzz, he saw the message got through. We always took care of our own. I caught him having a hamburger across the street from his corner spot and climbed up on a stool next to him. "What have you got, Pete?" I ordered coffee and when it came, sipped it slowly.

"You pull some big ones, Irish. Good thing you got friends. Remember Millie Slaker?"

"She still hustling?"

"Yeah. So she leaves a client where they dumped the ambulance. She seen this guy get out and walk back to the corner where another car was waiting. Millie, she's in a doorway by now because she don't like the setup, but she hears the guy tell the other one to stop at the Big Top for something to eat before they go back. Millie got outa there then and that was that, but I checked the Big Top Diner and Maxine Choo remembered them because they was both foreigners. Now Maxine's a Hunkie, but she still picks up enough Polish to get the drift of their talk and hears them mention Matt Kawolski's place down by the bridge. They was both arguing about something like if they should check in and pick up expenses right then or wait. She got kind of busy then and when she listened back in they had decided, paid up and left.

"I sent Benny down to talk to Matt but with all the seamen dropping in his place he couldn't tell who was new and who wasn't, besides half the guys there never spoke English anyway, and Matt, he's too damn busy to bend an ear to somebody else's chatter."

I said, "Get a description from Millie?"

"What am I, dumb?" he asked indignantly. "Sure. The guy she made was average all around and you couldn't pick him outa a crowd except he had only half an ear. Maxine didn't see that side of him, but the other guy she said was a mug type. Tough, broken nose, that kind of jazz. You know?"

"It's enough."

"So you goin' down there?"

"Tonight. Keep some of our people around."

"Sure, they're on the street. They won't let up until I call 'em off, don't take too long. They still have bucks to make and it ain't easy. This convention crowd is a tight bunch with their loot pinned to their pockets."

I looked at my watch. "It has to be fast." I threw a buck on the counter to cover the bill.

Pete-the-Dog suddenly grabbed my arm. "Hey Irish, Big Step softening up?"

"What do you mean?"

"Carney said he took his spotter off Fly's joint. Maybe he ain't out for poor Fly no more. All the time he had that punchy Martino staked out to nail Fly if he went home and now Martino is gone."

I started to put the pieces together and they fit nicely. When Tarbush opened he would have seen Fly's body and gotten to Ernie South. With the cache of H gone they wouldn't have time to play any fancy tricks, so with Big Step's help they must have rigged it to get Fly back to his pad and let him be found there. Nice trick in the daytime, but it could be worked. Right now Ernie must be flipping with his supply of narcotics gone. I wished I had had time to shake down the place completely.

I said, "No, he's not getting soft. See you later."

"Sure thing."

The darkness had closed in completely by the time I

reached Matt Kawolski's place. It was a dirty joint on the corner across the street from the river that stunk of city sewage from the vents in the area, stale beer and just plain age, but it was in a handy spot for everybody from the day crew at the nearby newspaper to the night crowd of seamen, bums and escapees from a city housing project a few blocks away. I hadn't been there in five years so I wasn't worried about being recognized, and Matt wouldn't even tip his own mother to an old face.

I managed to snag Matt alone in the back kitchen and I didn't have to paint any pictures for him. Before I could ask he said, "Blue station wagon and a late model sedan parked outside Mort Gilfern's print shop. He don't get much action never."

"He the one that turns out that Commie newssheet?"

"Yeah, hands it out free to the seamen. Plays up trouble, goes for ship tieups, backs hardnosed union demands. I won't let him in here since he was in the May Day parade. Says he's a liberal, but I know what he is."

"How'd you hear?"

"Billie Cole said it." He threw a quick look to the half closed door and wiped the sweat from his face. "That guy with the half a ear . . ."

"What about him?"

"Billie saw him gettin' out a car. He been there before, Billie said."

"Thanks, Matt."

"You gonna bring any trouble in here?"

"Nope."

"Can if you want. Enough boys here to take care of it. They ain't all alike. Some of you guys from uptown are scrounging around too."

"I'll yell if I need them."

"Since when did you ever need anybody?" he asked and went back to cleaning out his pots under a steaming faucet.

The rain had turned from a drizzle to a hard, slashing downpour. The fog had dispersed, but the cloud bank overhead put a ceiling on the city like sealing up a tomb. Small rolling rivers cascaded along the curbs to swirl down into the sewers and aside from a hissing of occasional car tires on the wet streets, all sound had been obliterated. Even the short blasts from tugs in the river or freighters at the docks were muffled and the jets circling overhead to come in at LaGuardia or International had no more than the soft drone of a bee then were gone.

Nobody was on the street. If they were, they had slouched back into doorways or found a dry spot in one of the abandoned buildings if they couldn't afford a beer inside a gin mill somewhere. I came out of Matt's alone, trench coat open, hat half sideways on my head, weaving up the sidewalk like any early drunk, oblivious of the downpour. In case anyone was watching I even managed to make myself sick and chucked my cookies up against a wall. It was a nice act. It got me past the old store where Mort Gilfern had his print shop and time to case it quickly. The windows were painted over and I knew the door would be locked, but through a chip in the lettering that spelled out Mort's name I saw a speck of yellow that meant he had a light on inside.

There was no back way in. The opposite street was a clutter of construction equipment and piles of rubble where buildings had been demolished with the debris still in gigantic piles waiting to be hauled off. A well lighted watchman's shack was on the site and inside a pair of uniformed guards were looking out the side doors.

One was still open and I took it. I scaled a fence on the other end, forced down a rusted fire ladder and swung myself up to the landing. The stairs leading to the roof were all but rusted through and I stayed tight to the edge where the support was greatest. They were all three story buildings, most of them empty, with evidences of summertime love nests here and there, rotted army cots and soggy mattresses with empty wine bottles thrown carelessly aside. I went over the parapets, keeping to the shadows until I was on top of the building that housed Mort Gilfern on the bottom floor. Ahead of me in the night was the irregular outline of the rooftop entrance.

Mort hadn't taken any chances. It was a steel fire door and bolted from the inside. The plating over it was fairly new and bolted in place. Unlike the other buildings, this one had no skylight. The only way down was the fire escape, a steel vertical ladder hugging the exterior wall fifteen feet to the landing and anyplace along it I would be a perfect target. I hated to lose the trenchcoat, but it was too light in color. I shucked it off and left it on the rooftop. In my black suit I would be almost impossible to spot unless a light hit me squarely.

The rain went through my clothes before I was halfway down. I made the landing and stood there a minute. Beside me a dirty window was locked in place, pigeon droppings and a mound of coal dust and grit piled along the sill showing it hadn't been used in months. I started to feel my way down the staircase to the next floor when I saw the thin line of light that reflected on the sandstone basement and then the lightning flash cut through the cloud layer above and I froze. The thunder came immediately afterward, a dull booming that preceded a sharper crack. I was glad I had the chance to immobilize myself there. Down below I saw the faint red dot that brightened once, the tip of a cigarette that flared as the guy behind it sucked in hard.

Between the bursts of light I went back up to the top landing, waited for the flash, and when the thunder followed it, rapped a hole in the window pane and hoped the sound wasn't heard below. It only took a second to open the latch and get the window up, then I was inside. These old buildings were built from identical patterns to exact minimum specifications and I had no trouble feeling my way to the stairwell outside the door. I went down the steps, sweating out each creak, pausing between sounds until I was on the second floor.

The door on my left was shut, but the warp in it bowed it inwards and the light in the gap showed no sign of a chain across it. I knew they'd have it locked but that wouldn't be any trouble at all. It would have to be quick and it would have to be exact. There wouldn't be time for second chances. These were pros trained in a school that specialized in perfection and they wouldn't be just sitting there idly.

As softly as I could I edged up close, the .45 cocked in my fist. Inside there was a choked sob and a harsh voice said abruptly, "Be still!" There was a foreign rasp to his words I couldn't quite place.

There was another sob and I knew I had guessed right. It was a woman and it could be only one. This time it was the other voice that said in the same accent, "Lady, I will make you be quiet!"

He might have. I heard a chair scrape back when the other one rattled something off in what sounded like Polish and at the same time I blasted the lock off the door with the .45 and smashed the door wide open with my foot so that it splintered with a dry crack and dangled from one hinge.

They spun together and I had time to see that only one had a gun beside him on the tabletop. I blew his whole face into a bloody froth with the first shot and as the other one unlimbered a Luger from his belt already thinking he had me I took him through the chest dead center and he half flew backwards across the room as he screamed *"Alex!"* just once. He was dead before his head made a sodden sound against the radiator and I didn't stand there waiting. I triggered three shots fast into the floor, backed out into the hall, listened a minute and went down the stairs fast and waited.

Maybe it took ten seconds, maybe less, but I was there first. The one who had been outside came in with all the stupidity that initial excitement brings on and forgot the rules. He remembered them a moment too late and by then he felt the gun in the back of his neck and his knees went limp with fear because he knew there was no sportsmanship in this game and he would be dead before he could move.

I said, "Upstairs," and went behind him, the .45 barely nudging his spine right above his belt. He let out little whining noises and when he saw the two on the floor he gagged, spilling his supper down the front of his suit.

Karen Sinclair lay on a rumpled bed still wrapped in a white hospital gown. A dirty blanket was thrown carelessly over her legs and her hands were taped together on her stomach. Both ankles were taped too, the strip running around the metal framework of the bed.

Someone had wanted to see what she looked like and the gown was pulled up to her navel. She was conscious now, her eyes wide open . . . and now she was beautiful. I kept the gun on the guy, pulled the gown down, flicked open the blade I carried in my pocket and sliced through the tape around her wrists and ankles. She smiled, never taking her eyes from me.

Very slowly then I turned and looked at the face of the one who had been outside.

Their eyes always got that way when they knew they were about to die. It was a dull, glassy look and a slack expression and no words because they realized that the one on the other end of the gun had the same conscience factor as they had themselves and would shoot for the fun of it if they had to. They could hardly talk with the fear, so they couldn't lie at all. They could only hope that it would be over fast and painlessly and not with a gigantic hole in their intestines that would leave them living in hours of agony before the merciful blackness came.

I said to him, "Manos Dekker . . . where is he?"

A long string of saliva drolled from his mouth. He turned his head and looked at the mess on the floor. Outside there was another flash of lightning, closer this time, and the sharp roll of thunder "He . . ." The guy stopped there, thinking about the rules again. He swallowed, wiped his mouth and let his lips come shut.

I lifted the gun and let him look down the big hole.

He saw it. He saw the hammer back and he could smell the cordite and the blood in the room. He said, "He went back to get . . . the thing."

"Where?"

And I knew he was telling the truth when the fear came back and he opened his hands helplessly. The fear was too big to let him lie, the smell of blood too strong.

I reached out and turned him around. "Look at that one," I said.

Automatically, he looked down at the corpse on the floor, the one without any face left at all. Then I swung the .45 and laid it across the side of his head so hard the scalp split and blood and tissue splashed over my hand. He went down without a sound, falling so that he was almost kissing the faceless body of the one by the radiator.

I went back to Karen and said, "Did they hurt you?"

"No . . . not yet. They . . . were waiting."

"Can you walk?"

"I can try."

"Maybe I can carry you."

"It won't be necessary."

"We have to get out of here. It isn't over yet."

She looked down at herself, gradually swinging her legs over the edge of the bed until she was sitting up. A grimace of pain went across her face, then disappeared.

"Wait a minute," I told her. I jacked a shell in the chamber of the Luger I took from the guy, threw it to her and raced up the stairs to the rooftop and unbolted the steel fire door. I found my trenchcoat where I threw it behind the parapet and took it back down again.

Women. They are all alike. Death they could face up to, public nakedness . . . never. She gave me a wry smile as I helped her into it, then followed me down the stairs. We went through the print shop and I unbolted the door so the others would have no trouble. I found the phone, dialed Shaffer's number and got him after I identified myself. He said, "Where are you, Irish?"

"Down under the Brooklyn Bridge, a place called Mort Gilfern's Print Shop."

"We know it."

"Then hit it. There are two dead guys and a cold one here waiting."

"Did you do it?"

"All by myself, buddy. I have news for you too."

"Oh?"

"I'm shaggin Karen Sinclair out of here too."

"Damn you, Irish, you . . ."

I chopped him off fast. "You asked for this, friend, so I'm doing it my way."

He was still swearing at me when I hung up.

Going the eight blocks before I found a taxi wasn't easy. I had to stop a dozen times and let her rest, my arm around her waist. Beneath my hands she was a warm, live thing, big and beautiful, the gutsy type I knew she would be and each time she stiffened and I knew she was hurting bad I felt the pain myself.

The taxi took us up to the Woolsey-Lever and I went through the lobby with her, both of us putting on an act. The rain had soaked her hair into a lovely wet backdrop against her face and her laugh was a tinkly thing I hadn't heard before. The fag behind the desk gave us an obnoxious glance and returned to answer the switchboard with a sniff of disdain, paying no attention as we got into the automatic elevator.

I got her upstairs, into the room and laid her down gently on the bed. I undressed her then, throwing the trenchcoat and hospital gown over the back of the chair. Both the bandages were showing a little seepage of blood through the gauze and when I pulled the sheet over her she grinned through the hurt and let her eyes close.

Naked, she was too beautiful. Even a deliberate attempt to disguise it couldn't last long at all. I couldn't look at her too long, didn't dare touch her, and hated anyone that ever saw her like I was seeing her now.

"Can you wait for me?"

She opened her eyes, made a smile again. "Forever if I have to," she said. "How do they call you?"

"Irish."

"No other name?"

"Ryan."

"What are you going to do now, Irish?"

"I'd hate to tell you. Sleep."

"Yes, Irish," I arranged the coverless pillow under her hair and let her fall back gently.

Someplace in the city another person was waiting to die. He didn't know it yet, but he would. I knew what

'The Thing' was . . . and I knew where 'back' would be.

And now I didn't need any more help.

With her eyes closed she said, "Irish . . ."

"What, honey?"

"The only . . . record . . . of where those missile pads are . . ."

"Yes?"

"In that capsule. It would take . . . six months to . . . locate them again . . . and it will be too late by then. I . . . can't tell . . . our people."

"That's what I thought. Don't worry about it."

I caught the barest glimmer of light from her pupils as she looked at me. "I won't."

Chapter 7

I LOVED the night. It was part of me, rain and all. It was an environment suited to me personally like it had been tailored that way and I put it around me like a cloak. I waved down a cab that was letting out a couple across the street, hopped in and gave him a street corner two blocks below Fly's pad. As we passed the Paramount building I looked up and checked my watch. It was a little after one.

Somehow the rain took on a new intensity, battering against the cab. The wipers worked furiously as if they were trying to claw through the downpour. I passed a buck over the driver's shoulder and got out, waited until he left and walked the rest of the way in total solitude. It was coming down too hard for anyone to be on the streets at all, even to look for a taxi and that's the way I wanted it.

The place where Fly had lived was in the basement rooms of a brownstone tenement, ugly places that were born with New York and now stood like decayed teeth in the jaws of the city. Cars were parked, nose to bumper along the curb, some junk heaps, others new and expensive from the newer apartments a few blocks away, the owners grabbing any available parking space as close as they could get to home. They would be lucky if they had tires left tomorrow.

I made my pass of the place from the opposite side, then crossed over and came back. I could be a target from a rooftop or window but I had to take the chance. There wasn't enough time left to case it thoroughly. When I reached the building I didn't hesitate, I took the short flight of stairs in two jumps, held in the shadows a second, then pushed the battered grill door back. I listened, but the noise of the rain didn't let any other sound filter through. The other door was already open, held against the wall with a brick.

With the .45 pushed ahead of me I went inside, feeling my way along the wall until I came to Fly's door. As carefully as I could, I turned the knob, nudged the door gently so that it eased back until it touched the arm of a chair and stopped. The only light in the room came from

134

the street lamps outside, an ineffectual pale amber reflection barely able to reach through rain and filthy glass panes.

But it was enough. Fly's body was there, all right, his neck still at that strange angle.

It was more than enough too because it let me see the other body stretched face down a few feet away almost hidden in the deeper shadows of a sofa.

I stood there, crouched to one side of the door jamb, letting my eyes become accustomed to the gloom, ears straining to catch any sound. Little by little I could see the ruin of the place, the sliced open furniture, the scattered junk all over the floor.

No, the job had been done. Two dead men and a ransacked apartment meant that they had come and gone. I stepped inside, walked to the other body on the floor and turned the head to one side.

It was Big Step's watcher, Martino. I put my foot under him and flipped him over. Whoever had placed the knife into him had done the neatest, most professional job I had ever seen. It had been expertly thrust and Martino had been dead without ever knowing it. A few glassy-eyed steps maybe, but that was all. It was the kind of thrust and tear wound only a trained expert like Manos Dekker could deliver.

When I looked around the place I saw the similarity of pattern there. It was like the back of Tarbush's Coffee Shop, every available hiding place being torn apart in the search, nothing missed.

And nothing found, either. The shakedown had started at one side and gone to the other, winding up at the door beside the upturned table. I grinned to myself because I knew it wasn't too late yet. That capsule was still hidden somewhere. Manos Dekker might know where ordinary people would stash a hot item, but he wasn't dealing with ordinary people. He was up against a hophead guarding his most valued treasure, his security against slow death.

I stood in the middle of the room and peered through the semi-darkness, objects beginning to become apparent. Dekker had done most of the work for me already. It didn't take much more. There was hardly an item that hadn't been ripped or smashed, taken apart minutely in the futile search.

There wasn't much to it really. Too many addicts used the same gimmick, each thinking they had pulled an original trick. I picked up the cheap ceramic lamp whose hollow base had been smashed open, knocked the dented shade off and looked at the bulb. It was unbroken, but not screwed all the way down. I gave it a couple of turns and it came out in my hand. The capsule so many people had died for was there inside the socket. I dumped it out and held it in my hand.

Behind me Big Step said, "Don't move, Ryan. Not one move or you have a hole in you big enough to throw a cat through. Lay that rod on the table. Easy."

And now it was over. All the way. The muscles under my skin were bunched and jumping and I knew there wasn't any use trying for the long shot. All I could do was stay alive as long as I could. I let the capsule dribble between my fingers unseen and heard it roll on the floor. Very elaborately, careful to let him see how I was doing it, I laid the .45 on the table and turned around.

Big Step wasn't alone. Ernie South was right next to him with a gun in his hand too and the smile he wore said I was ripe for dying any second. Step bumped Ernie with his elbow. "Close those curtains on the window."

Ernie nodded, walked around me and yanked the cord on the venetian blinds, then pulled the drapes over them. The dust came out in a small cloud and I thought for a second I might be able to move in the almost total darkness. But Step thought of it too and flipped the light switch on before I had the chance.

"I knew you'd come back, Irish. I knew you'd sucker yourself right into my hands."

"So I'm a jerk."

"A big one. We were waiting upstairs." He grinned at me slowly, his hate filled eyes black with a wild passion. "Killing Fly was stupid, Irish. You think you could tie us into it by letting him stay at Tarbush's? Ernie and me, we got him back here and when you put a shiv in old Martino you even did us a favor. So the cops make it out like Fly stuck him and he had a chance to break the creep's neck before he died."

"Where's the knife, Step?" I asked casually.

"Come off it, punk. Who cares? We'll put another one in the hole." He moved away from the door and sat back on the arm of the old wooden chair by the wall. "So you catch Fly raiding Ernie's warehouse. You figure he got more tucked away here and come looking for it, only you gotta kill Martino first." He gave a slow glance around the room, then back to me. "Fly did a damn good job of hiding it, but if Ernie has to tear this place apart board by board, he'll find it. That's just too much loot to throw away. And me, I got what I want, Irish, I got you."

Ernie said, "He stashed those packets of H, Step. Don't you bump him until he talks." He looked at me, teeth bared with anger. "Or do you want to make it easy on yourself."

I shrugged, watching them both for any opening at all. "I don't have your junk."

"Suit yourself, buddy," Ernie said. "I'm going to enjoy playing with you." He got up and walked around behind me. I just started to swing when the butt of his gun smashed into my skull with a crack I barely heard before all sight and sound disappeared into a maelstrom of ink and I felt myself falling from a great height.

How long it was, I couldn't tell. I came to with a rush of sudden pain that swept down from the top of my head and invaded my whole body. My hands and legs were behind me and when I made a spasmodic move there was a tug at my neck and a cord tightened there almost shutting off my breath.

Big Step still sat there, smiling pleasantly, enjoying the scene. "The Capone loop, Irish. Every move makes it tighter. Soon you'll get a cramp and you'll be able to feel yourself die inches at a time."

"Where is it, Irish?" Ernie South asked me.

I let out a strangled sound and shook my head. What a damn fool I was! Big Step was right when he called me a sucker. I try it alone and blow the whole bit including myself. A woman I wanted and a whole world might die because I was a damn idiot. All I had to do was make a phone call.

Big Step got up, pulled the chair around so he could watch me and sat down in it, his legs stretched out in front of him. "Take it slow, Irish. This is for Penny and Little Step. My brothers." A look of pain crossed his face. "They was kids, Irish. You got them both dead. However the hell you worked it, I don't know, but you got them dead and you're paying." He glanced over at Ernie and said, "If he goes out loosen up that cord and start him over again. We got plenty of time."

Ernie nodded agreeably. "He'll start talking a couple times around."

"Sure he will, won't you, Irish? You'll tell Ernie what you did with his stuff then I'll kill you quick for killing Penny and Little Step."

The voice from the door said, "He didn't kill Penny, Step." I couldn't move an inch except for my eyes. Ernie and Big Step both make quick moves toward their belts, but stopped halfway there. Leaning up against the door jamb with a flat black automatic in her hand was Lisa Williams and she was gassed to the ears, a drunken smirk twisting her mouth in a crazy smile, her eyes glassy, her hair in wet strings down her head. The broken nose, the scars on her face stood out lividly, giving her a frightening appearance.

Both Ernie and Big Step looked at each other, not wanting to take a chance with a drunk with a gun, but it was Big Step who spoke first, just trying to make enough conversation to get her off guard. "What you say, Lisa?"

"Irish didn't kill your brother, Step, but I'm going to kill you. I promised myself that a long time ago, and now I'm going to do it." She eyed the two bodies on the floor, looked briefly at me and her lips pulled into a taut snarl. "You had to kill Fly and him and now you want to kill Irish too. You damn louse."

"Look you drunken bum . . ."

"You didn't have to kill Fly, Step."

He half rose from the chair. "Put that rod away, Lisa. This punk here bumped Fly. You think I . . ."

"Sit down, Step." She pointed the gun at his middle, but still keeping Ernie in view. "You don't have to tell me anything. I can see for myself. I know things like I know who killed Penny."

Big Step scowled, seemed to crouch in the chair. "Who, Lisa?"

"Ernie South here." She looked across the room at him and gave a silly laugh.

Big Step's frown deepened and he turned to stare at Ernie. "What the hell's she talking about?"

I could see Ernie, too. He was sweating. "She's drunk," he blurted.

"Sure I am," Lisa told him, "But I know. You think he was Penny's friend? Like hell he was. You handed over territory to Penny he wanted for himself and he hated Penny's guts. He got him out all right. All he had to do was wait and when Penny went for Irish with his big mouth and what he was going to do, Ernie killed him."

The sweat was really there now and Big Step saw it too. He let his eyes slide from Ernie back to Lisa and asked, "How'd you find out?"

"Fly told me."

Ernie stood up in a rage, his hands trembling. "A god-damn hophead tells a drunk and you listen to her? What kind of . . ."

"I think it makes sense, Ernie," Big Step said. "I heard noises like that from the boys. Moe tried to tell me and so did Carl Hoover and I wouldn't listen, but I'm listening now." His hand moved closer to his belt when he turned back to Lisa. "How did Fly know, Lisa?"

She laughed again, never taking the gun off him. "He saw him. He was looking for him to hit him up for some H and saw him. He was saving the story until he wanted to put some real heat on Ernie for a big bundle, only now he'll never be able to do it." Her face changed slowly and tears ran down the side of her face. "You killed Fly like you did me and now you go, Step."

The flat look on Big Step's face I had seen before. It was a death look and it was aimed at Ernie South. The narcotics dealer went white as the powder he peddled and every cord in his neck stood out like fingers. "Damn you, Lisa . . . she's lying . . . she's . . ." He never finished. His hand streaked for the gun in his belt, found and fired it in a split second and doubled Lisa up in the doorway as the slug took her right in the stomach.

But the sound of it was lost in the bigger roar of Step's rod that bucked in his hand and put a hole in Ernie South's temple and drove him over the arm of the couch. He got up then, smiling like it was an everyday occurence, thumbed back the hammer and walked over to me. "Too bad, Irish, but I can't leave you here to talk, y'know?" He pointed the gun at my head and I closed my eyes.

The blast came, a sharp, flat crack and I felt the concussion on my cheeks. There was no pain, no sensation at all. I forced my eyes open, looked up, hardly able to breathe. Above me Big Step Stipetto was arching in the final dance of death, his eyes staring in disbelief, the hole that went through his neck from back to front pumping blood furiously until the torn spinal cord got its last message through to his brain and he crumpled in a heap, dead.

In back of him Lisa still held the smoking automatic in her hand, every muscle in her body wracked with pain.

I couldn't tell her. I had to hope she could see what had to be done. And it was her still present hatred of Big Step that made her do it before she died. She had to undo anything he had done and somehow she inched across the floor until she reached me and I felt her fingers fumble the loop from my neck. With her last remaining energy she unknotted my wrists, smiled wistfully and fell back.

"Thanks, honey," I said, and touched her face gently. I let the feeling come back in my hands and finished untying my ankles. When it was done I knelt down beside her. "Don't move, kid, I'll get a doctor."

She let her eyes come open and the drunkness was gone from them now. There was a new look in its stead. "No use, Irish. It's better this way."

"Lisa . . ."

"Kiss me goodbye, Irish?" Somehow there was no smashed nose, no scars, and she looked like she must have when she was a Broadway star. Gently, I leaned down, touched my lips to hers, then her face relaxed while I watched her and she took her last curtain call.

I found the capsule where I dropped it, wrenched it apart and made sure the microfilm was still there, then put it back together and stuck it in my pocket. Outside I heard the wail of sirens and cut for the door. I had to beat the cops out or I'd be held sure as hell and the big killer was still loose. I pulled the grill back, started up the steps when the wall powdered beside me and I heard the crack of a gun from across the street. I was pinned there with no chance of breaking out and the first squad car came to a screaming halt at the curb. I took the cap out of my pocket, dropped it in the cuff of my pants and waited.

Newbolder and Schmidt didn't want to believe me. Five corpses were in the room and I was there alive with a .45 in my belt and to them it was all cut and dried. They had me where the hair was short and were enjoying it. But it was the move with the packets of heroin that turned the trick. When I asked Newbolder who he thought mailed them in and why, he stopped Schmidt's impatient move to get me in a squad car and said, "Keep talking, Irish."

"Not me. There's no time. You just get a call through on your radio." I gave him Shaffer's number and said, "Your office will know who it is. If you tie me up now there will be hell to pay tomorrow."

Schmidt grabbed my arm. "Let him do his talking downtown."

"No, wait a minute," Newbolder said. "This whole thing's screwy enough right now and I don't want to go on a chopping block when we can clear it now. You keep him here." He looked at Shaffer's card in his fingers thoughtfully and went outside through the crowd to his car.

He took about five minutes and when he came back his face was screwed up into a puzzled mask and he was shaking his head. "How the living hell do you do it, Ryan? How the hell do you work it?"

Schmidt said, "What's the pitch?"

"Later, I'll tell you later. Let him go."

"Are you nuts?"

"No, but you will be if you don't keep your hands off. Okay, Ryan, take off. Tomorrow we'll get a report. A personal one. I'll want that whole agency staff present with every document of authorization they have to make this one stand up. I want to hear this from front to end and get it in writing so I can read it every time I think there's an angle I don't know about. Now get your tail out of here to wherever you're going before I change my mind and take a chance of being caught in the wringer." He handed me the gun with a look of disgust and I walked out. Before I hit the street I got the capsule back and stuck it in my pocket.

I didn't wait for the elevator. I went up the stairs to my floor and half ran down the corridor. Then I stopped. The door stood open an inch and when I shoved it back I could see the whole interior of the room in the bright light from the overhead, bed and all.

Karen Sinclair was gone.

I walked in slowly, stood looking at the open window that led out to the fire escape, then switched off the light. The wind had changed direction and a sheet of rain came through and whipped across the floor. I peered out into the night, swearing at the blackness for the first time. They had time and they had the room. I had been delayed long enough for the snatch to be made and there was no way in the world of telling where they had taken her.

I slumped down on the bed, my face in my hands, trying to figure it out. Somehow I had left a trail in the hotel and they picked it up. But how? Damn it, I wasn't that sloppy. I had been the route too many times. One mistake somewhere along the line. That was all it took.

How long I sat there I couldn't tell. The floor and end of the bed was soaked, my shoes and pants legs drenched. Then the phone rang. Unconsciously, out of habit, I picked it up. "Hello." The voice didn't sound like my own at all.

"Good evening," the other one said. The voice was harsh with a curious accent, the tone inviting like it was waiting to be asked to tell a huge joke.

I sat up slowly, feeling the chill run down my back. "Manos Dekker," I said.

"You are a hard man to kill," he told me pleasantly. I waited, not trusting my voice. "You have something I want. I have something you want. I believe a trade is in order."

I went to answer him and a pair of clicks, a piece of a word interrupted the connection before it was reestablished and I said, "I'll deliver. How?" I had no choice. No choice at all.

"Ah, that is very good. Then we shall arrange it."

"Let me speak to her first. I'm not paying for a dead body."

I knew she'd be alive. He'd know I'd insist upon it. He called out, speaking away from the phone and once again the connection was interrupted for a split second, then I heard her voice saying, "Don't do it, Irish."

Manos Dekker laughed softly to himself. "Oh, he will do it all right. He is a very decent American. He is like all the others of his kind. Very sentimental."

"Okay, Dekker, you call it."

"Yes, I will," he laughed again. "I will call you back within minutes and tell you what it is you have to do. I wouldn't advise any interference in the matter. You understand, of course?"

"I understand," I said, my voice cold with the fear in it. He hung up before I did and I put the receiver back slowly.

There was a flaw somewhere. I could feel it. I had it in my hand if I could figure it out. I took it apart piece by piece, bit by bit, going over the picture from the minute I met Karen, remembering every detail of the action.

It took a while, but I got it.

Now I knew where she was and how I was going to work it.

I jacked a load into the breech of the .45, thumbed the hammer back and went out to the elevator and took it down to the lobby. The little fag at the desk had his back to me answering a call on the PBX board when I reached him. I went around the counter and put the gun against his spine and watched him stiffen. He turned around, his face a ghastly gray, his lips quivering as he saw my face.

"You Commie bastard," I said.

"Please . . ." he lifted his hands defensively.

"How'd they get you in . . . use sex appeal? Or was it your hate for everybody in the world in general."

"I . . . I'm not . . ."

"Shut up. I saw a photo of you in a special file the Feds have on all Commie sympathizers. It was taken a while ago and you weren't in half-drag and without the usual makeup you didn't quite look the same, but I put it together. You even helped. You cut in on my talk with Dekker because you were scared stiff and loused up your connections at the switchboard there. When Lennie Ames mentioned my name you reported in like a good stoolie. They told you I was hot and where I stood and you were the pipeline. You saw me bring the girl in and got to them right away and they set the deal up right here on the premises. Cute, kiddo, real cute."

I let him see my best grin, all the teeth. I let him look at the snout of the rod and said, "She's in the hotel, buddy-boy, buddy-boy. I'm guessing she's in your room. Am I right?"

The look he gave me told me I was. I reached in his pocket, found the key. Number 309.

"Let's go," I said.

I wasn't in a hurry now. I was going to do this one easy and my way. We got out of the elevator, walked down the hall nice and slowly, the queer's knees dancing with fright. He was as bad as the worst of them in his own way and he was paying for it. I was willing to bet this wasn't the first operation he had been on and when he was checked out all the way he'd wind up with a dossier an inch thick and loaded with names. Too many people in the striped pants departments of Washington agencies played games with these types and wound up being patsies for a blackmail racket worked by the Soviets.

When we reached the door I eased the key in, the gun in his back telling the guy not to make a sound. I turned it, felt the latch go back and took the chance the chain was strung in place. Then I turned the knob, shoved the door open and rammed the desk clerk into the room with the flat of my hand.

He was quick, all right. The gun seemed to jump into his hand and the first shot took the clerk through the chest. And I had the time I needed. Manos Dekker saw the play and knew he couldn't make it and in a desperate attempt to wash it out the most horrible way he knew he whipped the gun in his hand toward the bed but before he could pull the trigger my .45 roared and blew the thing out of his hand, fingers and all. He looked at the bloody mess on the end of his wrist, no longer the killer he was, a fanatic with a political drive that matched his own lusts and made him a big cog in a big machine. He looked back at me, knew what was coming and tried to open his mouth to scream or plead or do anything to stop it. He opened his mouth wide and I shot him right through that gaping hole in his face and he slammed head first into the wall splattering his blood and brains all over the place.

Karen Sinclair looked up at me from the bed and smiled, her eyes bright and shiny. He hadn't done anything to her. He would have, but he hadn't. My luck ran just a little too good. I took out the capsule from my pocket and held it out. She opened her hand and I let it fall into her palm.

The way she looked at me and I knew I was looking at her said that it was just the beginning for the both of us. There was a long road to be walked and we'd be doing it together. The hood was gone because my own would never let me back again when the story came out and I had to walk the other side of the street whether I liked it or not. Shaffer didn't realize what he had gotten himself into.

Karen looked at the capsule in her hand as I bent down to kiss her. Her mouth was a full, wetly warm blossom that tried to envelop me, her tongue tasting me, one finger tracing a line along my face. I stood up and reached for the phone to dial Shaffer's number.

She said, "How many people are in New York, Irish?"

"Many millions, doll."

Karen looked at the capsule, then smiled at me, the beauty of her like starlight on a clear night.

"I knew I gave it to the right one," she said.